ACKNOWLEDGEMENTS

Again, a special thanks must go to my daughter Lesley without whose badgering, ruthless editing and support, my first book would never have been published and this book would have been just wishful thinking.

Thanks to Robyn Lines, the model for the cover.

Photographer – Mia Burt

Also, Robyn and Lesley for their constructive criticism.

Other books by Malcolm Colley

Zachariah: The Boer Diamond
Ichnasius: The Boer Gold
Jedidiah: The Boer Thunder
Dorothea: The Boer Treasure
Gideon: The Boer Blood
Black Smoke

Of Love and Lust

by

Malcolm Colley

INTRODUCTION

This is based on a true story, only the names and places have been changed to protect their identity. I say 'based on' because I have dramatized it, a lot.

As you can see from the title, it is about the difference between lust and love.

On some reflection and putting my thoughts together, I find I believe that each one of us has a flaw built into our character or body that we need to spend the whole of our lives wrestling with, whether it is being an adulterer (sleeping with another man's wife) or an alcoholic, or a kleptomaniac or a liar or even a murderer. I don't believe any one of them is greater than the other when it comes to the battle within. I know that I have my own demons to battle with.

Regardless of your belief system or religion, the Ten Commandments and The Seven Deadly Sins are good tools against which we can measure ourselves. The Ten Commandments are even used as a basis, in all western countries, for common law. I am adding them in below merely for convenience for recognizing the scene.

An extract from Wikipedia

*The **seven deadly sins**, also known as the **capital vices** or **cardinal sins**, is a grouping and classification of vices within Christian teachings. Behaviours or habits are classified under this category if they directly give birth to other immoralities. According to the standard list, they are **pride**, **greed**, **lust**, **envy**, **gluttony**, **wrath** and **sloth**. These sins are often thought to be abuses or excessive versions of one's natural faculties or passions (for example, gluttony abuses one's desire to eat).*

Evagrius Ponticus, identified seven or eight evil thoughts or spirits that one needed to overcome. Evagrius' pupil John Cassian, with his book The Institutes, brought the classification to Europe, where it became fundamental to Roman Catholic confessional practices.

The Ten Commandments are from the Jewish and Christian religion and are basically; Love your God completely and love your neighbour as yourself. On these two commandments hang all the rest. If you love your neighbour as yourself then stealing, murder, adultery, etc., will be taken care of.

These Commandments can be found in Exodus 20 of the Old Testament of the Bible.

So, if lying, anger, intolerance (all actions that go against the commandment of loving your neighbour) are sin and we know that sin bars us from heaven, then who can enter the kingdom of God? Well the secret is hidden in this story.

Now, our hero of our story broke so many of the commandments but in particular, do not commit adultery and do not covet your neighbour's wife, and even do not murder, that one would suppose that there was no way back for him.

This is not a history lesson nor a sermon (homily) but it does have a moral to it. Enjoy the story.

The wars in the background of the story are interesting and may have contributed to the circumstances but it could have been any wars, taking place anywhere. It could have been one of the many wars in England, America or even Israel. I have chosen South African history because I grew up there but if I had grown up in Arizona, USA the wars would be different, maybe against the local American Indians, but the story would remain the same. Of importance is the story of lust and the story of love.

You can skip the explanation of the wars, if you wish. It won't make any difference to the story.

There were three wars that were fought during the period of my story; The Pedi War, the First Boer War and the Second Boer War.

THE PEDI BACKGROUND

The Boers and the Pedi were always at loggerheads in the area later to become the Eastern Transvaal and later still, Mpumalanga. As early as 1852 Hendrik Potgieter decided to end the conflict by besieging the Pedi stronghold under Chief Sekwati. The siege was unsuccessful but Potgieter came away with Sekwati's cattle. Sekwati eventually signed a treaty with the Boers and agreed to a border at Steelpoort River.

Sekwati died in 1861 and his two sons, Mampuru and Sekhukhune, became rivals for his throne. Sekhukhune declared himself ruler and Mampuru went on the run and sought refuge amongst the neighbouring Ndebele.

By 1879, conflict again broke out against both the Boers and the British. Sekhukhune was first captured by the British but in 1881 was released by the Boers. He was murdered by his brother Mampuru. Mampuru was later captured and executed in Pretoria.

THE FIRST BOER WAR

The first war between the Boers and the British kicked off in 1880. By then the Pedi were down to a few farm raids and the Zulus had been defeated. The Boers found that in the interim, the British had decided that they were now the big-wigs in the Transvaal. Some say it was because of the discovery of diamonds in the western Transvaal. The war was sparked by a fight over a wagon that the British tried to seize from a Boer who wouldn't pay his taxes. It ended with a humiliating defeat of the British at Amajuba in 1881.

THE SECOND BOER WAR

As far as the Boers were concerned, the British were over-stepping the line with their wanting to annex the Transvaal and generally thinking that they could lord it over everyone. The Boers had beaten them once and were confident they could do it again. Unfortunately, they underestimated the British might. At the start of the Frist War the British were ill-prepared but the defeat by the Boers spurred the British to start pumping soldiers into the country. At the start of the second war, the British were learning fast and the picture was totally different.

Of course, as with all wars, courageous men died. That is the inevitability of war, people die.

AND SO, TO THE STORY

It was during this time of unrest, after the murder of Sekhkhune, to begin with, that our story takes place. The Boers were on the offensive. Their commandoes were hitting the Pedis hard but the young, Pedi warriors were still stealing through the border of the Steelpoort River and attacking the farms.

The commandoes in the east were led by a fearless Commandant by the name of Johannes Venter. Son of a Dutchman but of an Irish mother, Irene Barron. He had first fiercely resisted the British rule. For his troubles he had been sent to Cape Town prison for seven years. His wife, Truida, thinking him dead, had remarried to Karl Shultz, a very influential man in the area, on advice of her father. Truida had two children by Johan, Trudi and Adrian. Johan was a brilliant leader of men, charismatic by nature and impressive in stature and looks. In the true story, his name wasn't Johannes Venter of course. A name does matter, it is a man's most prominent characteristic after all.

Karl was also a very rich man, very much in love with Truida. He loved the two children, because of his love for Truida but he was often disappointed that there were no blood children. He would bequeath all his riches to them though. Karl was more inclined to making money than war. I suppose that was part of the reason that, when Johannes was released from prison and returned to his farm, Truida wanted nothing to do with Johannes or Johan. People say she had turned into a money grabber but others say she saw that he had changed since their marriage.

CHAPTER 1

Johan tripled his horse, Blaau, forward. He had thirty of his best men behind him. They spread out as they came out of the trees. Ahead of them the Pedi warriors were chanting their war song, stamping their feet. Johan watched them spreading, raising his fist high. There must have been more than a hundred and some of them brought their old muzzle-loaders to their shoulders. The Boers held back, knowing that they were still out of range of the old guns. As the muzzle loaders fired, Johan brought his fist down for the charge.

The horses thundered across the grassy valley. The trick was to engage before the muzzle-loaders could be reloaded. At the same time, the Boers brought their newly acquired 7mm Mausers into action. With the bolt action, there was time for two shots to be fired before the clash. At least fifty Pedi fell but even so the Boers were outnumbered two to one. Some of the Pedi, directly ahead of them, turned and ran.

The horses ploughed through the ranks. Coming out the other side the Boers rode a short distance, giving them a chance to reload as they turned and charged again. In the next clash, Johan saw one of his men go down. He turned Blaau on his heel and jumped him toward the spot, swinging the butt of his rifle at the mass around him.

His man was up, hat off, head bleeding. Johan saw that it was Kobus, parrying a spear but taking a slice in his arm. Blaau, a blue-black stallion, trampled, nostrils flaring, a war horse like few. As Johan bent down, right arm extended to Kobus, he felt the hot slice of a spear across his far side hip. Kobus was up behind him and Blaau took them clear of the fighting.

By this time the Pedi were in disarray, breaking ranks and peeling off. When the rest saw what was happening, they also turned and ran. Kobus swung down. Johan made ready to follow the fleeing Pedi but first looked around to see the order of his men. Most were already working their bolts and positioning to take parting shots. Rifles thundered and men fell.

"Hold up!" Johan shouted holding his fist in the air again.

His men looked to him, waiting for orders. They rallied around him. Horses were snorting and shuffling back and forth. All faces were turned toward him. His men would've ridden into the mouth of hell with him.

"They have learnt a lesson today that they will remember for a while."

"I didn't see Mampuru amongst them," said Pieter. "I didn't recognise the leader."

"No," Johan agreed but then turned to look at his men. "How are we all?"

"Only cuts," said Kobus as he swung up behind Pieter.

Kobus's horse was standing a short distance off with its head down. Pieter turned and cantered toward him. Kobus slipped onto his own horse, patting and smoothing his neck.

"Ok, let's go home," said Johan, swinging his horse around.

Pieter and Kobus rode next to him as they cantered toward Kameelbult. Kameelbult lies forty km north-west of Lydenburg. The sun was dropping behind them and all the noises of the bush at sunset were surrounding them. Johan was keen to reach home without stopping to camp. He really felt triumphant. It had been a good day. The cuts that a number of the men had suffered should be seen to but there was nothing serious that needed attention immediately. No stab wounds that could cause problems.

Johan rode high in the saddle. He was striking in stature and regarded as handsome by all women and some men. A square jaw with a short black beard, built like a stone shed. Johan's high feelings dropped a bit when he thought about home. He didn't have anyone there to meet him and welcome him home. Truida, his wife, who he had loved, had now gone for good. Married to that conniving bastard. There were a few women who he found attractive.

In fact, there were two with whom he had slept before he had been captured and sent to prison in Cape Town by the British. Three children who he had fathered. A daughter and a son with Truida but he doubted whether even the mother knew that he was the father of his second son, the mother being married. Johan was a handsome man, there was no getting away from it. His sons took after him; not only in looks. He also had the heightened sexual drive that usually goes with the charismatic character of a great leader.

Nobody knew about his first wife, Michelle. Married too young, she was only sixteen and he was eighteen. Michelle had said she loved Johan and even saved his life on one occasion but that was before he had become religious. She had finally left him because he wanted to join the local Dutch Reformed Church and even actually raised his arms in church. All this thinking dampened his spirits. He pulled his thoughts together, shouted into the night and cantered ahead punching the air. Pieter and Kobus, thinking he was shouting with joy, also shouted and joined him.

"I want to reach home tonight!" he called to those riding next to him. They nodded agreement and spurred their horses on. They chased up a flock of Guinea-fowl as they rode into the night. The moon was already being kind to them and lighting the road which looked like a silver ribbon. The sky was clear above them but lightning flashed on the horizon.

CHAPTER 2

The birds were heralding the dawn by the time they road into town. The storm had missed them, skirting to their left. Johan's house was on the far side of town overlooking the valley and he waved to his men as they peeled off to their homes. His house was dark and no-one greeted him. He led Blaau into the barn, stripped of the saddle and blanket and wiped him down with the towel hanging in the stall. He filled the trough with water and then walked to the house. His man-servant, Phineas, would see to Blaau when he came in at around seven. Phineas was Shangaan from across the border in Mozambique. The Shangaan were related to the Zulus and had nothing but contempt for the Bapedi.

Phineas had been with Johan since they were preteens, about ten years old. They had fought for and against each other. Johan had spoken Shangaan before he had learnt Dutch, his mother tongue. But Johan had come from a rich, white family and Phineas from a poor, black family so Phineas had ended up working for Johan but even if that hadn't been the case, Johan was the born leader. Phineas admired Johan as a leader and followed him without question

Johan hated being alone, with the house feeling so hollow and empty. Maybe he should get a dog. In the meantime, he was alone and that was it. He had even drifted away from his God. He was struggling to pray since he had arrived back from Cape Town and found Truida gone. Surely God wouldn't want him to be alone.

He stripped down to his under-pants and boots and walked out to the trough behind the house. No houses overlooked his so he wasn't worried about anyone seeing him but as he walked toward the trough, he heard soft singing coming from the river. It was difficult to see down to the river from his back yard, so he went into his barn and climbed to the loft. Trying to not let his boots make a noise on the wooden floor. From there he could look down on the river.

Standing in the river with water only up to her knees was Helena, his childhood sweetheart. She was naked. Her golden blond hair halfway down her back. He only just glimpsed her breasts before she turned so that he could only see her back. He tried to will her to turn around but it didn't work. She was singing a song that they used to sing as youngsters at Sunday-school. He could feel himself being aroused and knew he was doing wrong but it was difficult to turn away. It took all of his will-power to turn and climb down from the loft.

Helena had a slim figure, slightly shorter than Johan. A natural blonde, as Johan had witnessed. A slim figure wasn't really in fashion in those day but, to Johan, she was the most desirable thing in the world and he was ready to put his world in jeopardy right now.

Helena kept her back turned but she had caught movement out the corner of her eye. Once she had his image, she could feel his gaze burning into her. She knew who it was. It was her childhood sweetheart who had rejected her for another woman. She had remained in love with him. Now the thought that he was watching her aroused her. Life hadn't been easy for her, with her husband being away for so long. How could she not long for him or long for anyone's arms around her to comfort her at night. She had been very lonely.

The arousal built up in her and she allowed it to burn, thinking of turning around slowly so that he would see her from the front. She threw her hair to one side, slowly turning. She was so aroused by now that she nearly fell over but when she turned and looked up, he was gone. It took her some time to calm down enough to be able to climb the bank out of the river-bed.

The icy water from the trough, splashed over his body helped Johan to calm down but the image of Helena's body seemed to be burnt into his brain. The water caused the cut in his side to sting and reminded him that he should do something about it before it festered. He towled himself down as he walked back to the house, Helena's image was still with him.

He couldn't bother going to the Jew who, he knew, sold disinfectant powder to put on his wound so he made a poultice with honey on a rag and bandaged it around his waist. He had hardly finished dressing when he heard his woman-servant, Miriam, come into the kitchen and start rattling pots and pans.

Miriam was Matabelle, and although the Matabelle, Ndebelle and Bapedi were all from the same stem of Bantu, they didn't have any time for each other. Miriam had once had a shine for Johan but that was long over. She realised that he was out of reach to her.

Johan needed to get his mind functioning properly, "Morning Miriam," he greeted her as he walked into the kitchen.

"Morning Baas," half turning from the stove. "Would the Baas like some *pap*?"

Johan liked to share the maize-meal porridge with Miriam and Phineas in the morning. He wanted them to feel that they were more than just servants to him. They, in return, appreciated the gesture. It really wasn't the done thing in the community at that time and Johan knew that, even in Holland the same culture applied.

"The news is that the raid was successful yesterday?" Miriam said as Phineas came in through the back door.

Phineas took his hat off and sat at the end of the table. He loved his Baas, having known him since they were young. "Yes, I heard that too."

"News travels fast," said Johan, "but yes, it was."

Johan bowed his head said grace and they ate in silence for a while.

"Who lives in this house down here," Johan pointed toward the house next to the river. He tried not to sound too interested.

"The Burgers," answered Miriam. She stood up to pour coffee.

"The Burgers?"

"Yes, do you remember Helena?" Johan nodded.

"Well she married Uri Burger," said Phineas.

"Mmm, yes, I remember Uri. What is he doing now?" asked Johan.

"He is away with one of the commandoes, across Steelpoort," answered Phineas. "I heard that he is a fearless fighter."

Johan nodded as he stood up, trying to look uninterested. "I am going to sleep for a while, I didn't sleep at all last night. I may play the concertina for a while."

Miriam and Phineas both nodded and half stood as Johan walked toward his bedroom.

Johan was a very accomplished player of the concertina. He favoured the smaller English concertina over the German one. He played for a while, until he felt the comfort of sleep pulling him away. As he lay down on his bed, he tried to think of peaceful things so that he wouldn't think of Helena. He knew that, with her on his mind, he wouldn't get any sleep. It was difficult but eventually he managed to drift off.

CHAPTER 3

Trudi Venter was on her way to school. This was her last year that she would attend school. After all, she was a full-grown woman at sixteen years old. Her mother had left her real biological father seven years ago. Her mother, Truida, had said that it was because her father, Johan, had been unfaithful but Trudi thought that was only for an excuse to the church. Her step-father was rich and was good to her, showering her and her mother with gifts and a good easy life. She had no cause to complain but she would have loved to have had a closer relationship with her real father.

Trudi did have opportunity to see Johan and was allowed to visit him whenever she felt like it. Her older brother, Adrian, usually went with her to visit their father. Adrian was only older by two years and she knew that he was devoted to her. Johan always welcomed them and she could see that he did love them.

By the time she reached the school, her shoes had a thin layer of dust covering them so that they looked more brown than black. The dust on her shoes were like the concerns of this world covering our souls as we walk through life. Trudi was too young to think of things like that now, even though she did already have the concerns of a sixteen-year-old, Well, she was almost sixteen, in a few months anyway.

Rachel met her at the gate. Rachel was Jewish and her family spoke English at home but Rachel had learnt Dutch from the time she was a baby so she spoke Dutch as well as any of them. The language was changing though. "In the mouths of the people," her father had said. Her grandmother Shultz had scolded him for his words. To her grandmother, this change to the mother language was second only to blaspheming.

Rachel smiled wickedly and nodded toward the door of the school building, "he's watching you."

Abri was standing on the top step, smiling at them. He gave Trudi the chills. She didn't know why. Maybe because he was always looking for an excuse to hug them. He was as old as Adrian but still at school. He struggled a bit with his lessons and for this Trudi felt sorry for him and tolerated him but tried to keep a distance between them. She knew that Adrian didn't like him. It wasn't that Trudi disliked him. Being a bit slow in his lessons wasn't his fault. It was just this hugging thing that put her off his advances. Both her and Rachel had big breasts already and she had said to Rachel that he just wanted to pull their breasts against him.

Rachel was already a beautiful young lady with raven black hair. Some of the other kids didn't like to associate with Rachel because she was Jewish. People just referred to her father, who owned the only shop in town that sold dresses, as "the Jew". Trudi only knew that their surname was Davidson because she was her friend. Most people in town didn't even know that. They always said, "I bought my dress from the Jew."

They went into class and sat at their desk. Trudi sat at a three-seater and Rachel always sat next to her on one side and the other side was usually open. This morning Abri sat down next to her on the other side. She didn't mind too much but then he pushed his hip against her thigh. Trudi tried to move up and nearly pushed Rachel off the other side.

"Hey," Rachel exclaimed.

Abri's name was actually Abram but he didn't like that name because it sounded Jewish so he had always said that his name was Abri. He knew that he loved Trudi. There was something about her that attracted him to her. They even seemed to think alike when they were being given lessons in the classroom.

He was already full grown physically and brimming over with the juices of youth. His father said that he would still pick up the muscles of a man but he was already a strong boy. It wasn't that he didn't have good looks. The girls all agreed that he was handsome but they all had a weird feeling about him.

He became excited just by having his hip against Trudi's thigh. It felt as if his hip was on fire. It was hard to concentrate on what the teacher was saying. It was hard to concentrate at any time for him but, with this burning sensation, it was almost impossible. He did try to fight it. He knew that if he was called to stand up, he would embarrass himself. What he didn't know was that he had inherited this flaw in his character from his real father, Johannes Venter. Also, what he didn't know was that Trudi was his half-sister, same father.

After school, Abri followed Trudi for a while but she went to Rachel's house. The two of them laughing and giggling all the way home. Abri turned and slowly walked dejectedly to his house. He was wearing shorts. He hated shorts. They made him look like a young boy. He wanted to wear long trousers like his father. Adrian wore long trousers so why couldn't he. When he thought of Adrian, he could feel this red mist of dislike and anger descending on him. Adrian didn't have to go to school anymore and was treated like a man. He was even starting to go on commando with the men.

When he arrived at his house, standing at the gate was his best friend Martin Coleman. Martin was three years older than Abri and not even a proper

Dutchman. He was half English on his father's side. But he had grown up speaking Dutch so that helped, maybe.

When he saw Abri's downcast face his smile disappeared, "and now, what's wrong?"

"Ag nothing. I just love her so much," Abri answered shuffling with one foot in the dirt.

"Who?"

"Trudi Schultz or Venter, I don't know. She doesn't want to come near me."

"Does she speak to you?" questioned Martin.

"Yes, but she won't let me come near her. She always steps back when I try to hold her hand."

"Is it really worth the trouble just to hold her hand?" asked Martin.

Abri could feel himself becoming angry, "I want to do more than just hold her hand," he said.

Martin laughed.

"Don't laugh at me," said Abri, angrily.

"I'm not laughing at you," answered Martin, "I am laughing with you."

"Sometimes I think that it may be that Rachel girl who is telling her bad things about me.

Sometimes I think I can hear them gossiping about me."

"We could do something about that. We could tell Rachel that we will hurt her if she says bad things about you."

Abri liked that idea. It seemed to sooth his temper.

They walked together to the barn behind the house and sat in the shade of the Syringa tree behind the barn. They picked up small stones and threw them at the three piglets that were wandering around. The small stones weren't big enough to do any damage and they laughed as the piglets squealed and ran around.

"I have a good idea," said Martin after a while. "Tonight, when your mother comes home, tell her that you are feeling sick. Tell her that you heard that Trudi makes such good chicken soup that it makes sick people well again. Then ask her to tell Trudi to bring you soup here in your sickbed."

"Trudi won't do that," answered Abri, "she may make soup for me but she won't bring it to me."

"Or ask your mother to ask Johan Venter to tell her. I have heard that Johan is sweet on your mother."

Abri jumped up, "don't speak about my mother like that!" he shouted.

Martin just lay back and smiled. He wasn't scared of Abri even though Abri was bigger and even stronger than him. "Just do it," he said.

Abri slowly sat down again. Actually, it sounded like a good idea and, to tell the truth, he had seen how Johan and his mother looked at each other in church on a Sunday morning. He didn't know about Johan's attraction to anything in a dress.

The day stretched on and Adrian saw Abri and Martin coming out from behind the barn as he walked his horse up the street, coming from his step-father's cattle fields. Adrian didn't like either one of those two. Both a bit slow in the head but it wasn't that that made him dislike them. They always seemed to be up to no good. Nothing he could put a finger on but just a feeling. That *Engelsman*. Martin didn't seem to do any work. Always laying about and watching the girls as they came out of school.

Adrian's mind turned to the new revolver that his step-father had brought him from his trip to Pretoria. He had to admit, it was good to have a rich step-father. This revolver was really something special. It was a Schofield-Smith and Wesson .44 calibre. His step-dad had bought it from an American friend of his. It was one of the thousands of Smith and Wessons that had been made for the American civil war. Apparently, George Scofield had made modifications that had been adopted for later models. Adrian rode home with his new pride and joy tucked into his belt. He was very aware of it, not very comfortable but he was happier than he had been for a long time. It meant that he had to wear two bandoliers though, one for the .44 revolver shells and one for the 7mm Mauser shells.

His younger sister greeted him as he walked in the back door, walking with a small bag of flour she had fetched from the shed. He followed her into the kitchen and saw that his mother and sister were baking. He hugged them both before walking through to his bedroom, Abri and Martin forgotten. He tucked the revolver under a folded towel on a top shelf, Mauser in the corner and bandoliers hung up on a peg.

CHAPTER 4

Johan rested that day, apart from riding down to where his black-smith shop was pumping out smoke. Kleinjan, his black-smith was hammering away. The huge black man was wearing trousers and a leather apron, no shirt, and goggles with sweat pouring down his back. He wouldn't have heard Johan walk in but must have caught movement in the corner of his eye. He stopped working and turned with a big smile on his face. Kleinjan's son, who had been working the bellows, also stopped.

"*Nkosi,*" he greeted Johan. "I hear you had a good day yesterday." Kleinjan was Zulu and had no love for the Bapedi. He was proud of the stories that he had listened to as a young boy, of how the great Zulu king Shaka had almost annihilated the Bapedi years ago. He also considered Johan a great leader and wished this would be the end of that nation.

They got to talking about the job and Kleinjan showed Johan a steel rim that he was getting ready for a new wagon wheel.

The sun was setting as Johan road back toward his house. He wondered if Helena would be down at the river again. He hurried to the barn and climbed to the loft. He was almost too late to see her. She was coming out of the river in all her naked splendour, facing him this time. He nearly fell out of the loft with excitement. When he climbed down, he was sweating, he was aroused now to the point of not caring what the consequences of his actions would be. It was only the cold water of the trough that enabled him to finally fall asleep that night.

Was it all Helena's fault for what happened next? Had she seen Johan watching her? Some people argue that it was. She must have known that she could be seen. Of course she did, but the sin was his as much as hers.

Sunrise found him sitting on the stoop, just gazing into the distance, his concertina hanging loose in his right hand. Miriam saw him sitting there and came to ask him to come to the breakfast table. He wasn't hungry but went to the kitchen out of habit. Phineas and Miriam talked and tried to draw Johan into the conversation but Johan might as well have been a hundred miles away. He did eat but even his favourite food didn't satisfy him.

This was Truida's fault, he thought. With Truida by his side he wouldn't be wrestling with himself like this. He was starting to scheme at what he could do to get Helena into his bed. This was wrong, he thought, but he couldn't stop himself and didn't even think of praying for help. Praying would have helped. The burning desire blotted everything else out.

Phineas had left the house when Johan's Veldkornet, Pieter, the second in command of his Commando knocked at the front door.

Pieter had also taken more than one slice from a spear the day before, "how are you feeling," Johan asked him.

"No, I'm alright, and you?"

Johan grunted.

"What I came to tell you is that the Pedi have attacked oom Hannes' farm otherside the Steelpoort. We need to ride soon."

But Johan was already formulating a plan, "I have so much that I must organize here. You lead a commando against them. It shouldn't take you long. They are far from home. It should be an easy raid."

Pieter was quiet. It wasn't like Johan not to lead. These things that Johan had to do must be very important.

Johan looked at him, "can you do it?" he asked. "You have done it before."

"Yes, yes, of course," replied Pieter, looking away so that Johan wouldn't see the look on his face.

"Take Kobus with you," said Johan and they sat at the kitchen table, planning the raid.

The excitement was building in Johan. Would Helena be at her house? Would she come to Johan's house, if he asked her? What excuse would he give Miriam and Phineas, first to call her and then to get them away from his house. What was he going to say to Helena when she arrived? What would her reaction to his advances be?

It seemed like an eternity for Pieter to leave and, talking about eternity, was God watching him? But he was too wound up to think about such things. He pushed those thoughts out of his mind.

Finally, Pieter left. Johan stood on the stoop and watched him walk out the gate. He needed to call Phineas and Miriam. Miriam would be best to go call Helena but to what excuse? He was about to turn and walk back into the house when Jaqueline walked in the front gate. Johan groaned in his heart.

"Can I come in?" she asked.

His mind was screaming NO! "yes of course," he said.

He showed her into the house and through to the kitchen.

"How are you?" she asked, sitting down at the kitchen table. "I hear your raid was a success?"

It wasn't that he didn't like her. She was after all the mother of one of his sons and she was a good-looking woman. Once upon a time he had desired her too. It was just that his mind was on Helena right now.

"Yes, it was," he said, his mind wandering across to the house next door.

"The reason why I am here," said Jaqueline, "is that Abri is sick and is asking for the special, chicken soup that Trudi makes. Would you ask her to make some soup for him and take it to him at our house? He is in bed there."

Alarm bells should have been ringing in Johan's head. He knew that Abri was not very stable mentally, but Johan's mind was in another place.

"Ja, Ja," answered Johan, looking out of the window.

"Before you do anything else," she said, "he is very sick, you should visit him."

Johan pulled his mind back to earth. "Tell Trudi from me that she should do it."

"I will," said Jaqueline, as she stood to walk out the door, "but promise me that you will go and visit him.".

"Ok, ok," he said. Usually he would have walked her to the gate, but his mind was on Helena.

Johan watched Jaqueline walk down the garden path. She was wearing a white long dress that hugged her waist. Johan watched her posterior push against the cloth and move one to the other as she walked. He was really aroused now.

As soon as she was out the gate, he turned and called Phineas. "Go to the wheel shop," he said and help them there. They need to get that wheel fixed by tonight."

Phineas gave him a bit of a look before turning to go. Very strange, he thought. His baas had never sent him to help at the wheel shop before. Still, Baas was baas and he must do what Baas says. So, he collected his jacket (it could turn chilly in the evening) and strolled down the road. He was glad to get out a bit. Kleinjan looked at him strangely when he explained that it was Johan's idea that he help out.

He was scarcely out of the gate when Johan called Miriam. She had come back into the kitchen when Jaqueline and Johan walked out.

"Miriam, I want you to go call miss Helena. Tell her that I need to see her on a matter of importance," he said, as she walked in the door.

She also gave him a bit of a look before turning to go. Very strange, she thought. She had never known Baas Johan to want to speak to miss Helena.

"Oh!" he called after her, "and go to the Jew and buy some *muti* for me to put on this wound of mine." That would keep her away for a while.

Miriam came back in so Johan repeated what he had said, "and wait for him to make up the medicine properly before you come home."

Johan stood at the kitchen window waiting impatiently for Helena. It wasn't long before he saw her coming in the gate. She was wearing a light blue dress that sat tight over her breasts and middle. He hurried to greet her at the door. The arousal in Helena was burning ever since Miriam had come to call her

"Helena," he said, "I need to talk to you…" but she was already in his arms.

It was if she had been waiting for his call. It could be said that she may have known that he was watching her the previous evening and had, maybe, tempted him on purpose. She said later that a guinea-fowl had knocked the screen down, at the river. The screen that was supposed to shelter her from preying eyes. She had, after-all, been without a man for some time now and a woman also has needs.

Her legs wrapped around his hips as he walked her to the bedroom, their lips glued to each other. Even the men at the wagon workshop wouldn't have been able to pry them apart. They both groaned aloud, knowing that no-one would hear them. The day was hot, so it was natural that they would sweat and leave their clothes marked with moisture, so the clothes came off.

It didn't take long before both of them were satisfied and just as well because by the time Helena was walking out the front door, Miriam came walking in the gate. Helena was straightening her hair and pulling at her dress. What Johan didn't know and Helena hadn't thought of was that she had just finished her monthly time, that is why she had been down in the river. She was at her most prime.

Johan did go to visit Abri later that day. His encounter with Helena had calmed him slightly. Abri was lying on his bed, putting on a good show of feeling sick. Johan sat on a chair next to Abri's bed.

"Please ask Trudi to make me some soup," he pleaded, "my stomach is not right. Only her chicken soup can fix my stomach."

When Johan did finally speak to Trudi, he asked her to make some of her bread for Abri but Trudi knew that it was soup that Abri wanted. As a matter of fact, as we know, it wasn't soup that Abri wanted either.

CHAPTER 5

Rachel didn't notice Martin as she approached her father's shop. Her mind was far away, building castles in the sky, as young girls do.

He stepped in front of her, blocking her from the entrance, "I want to warn you," he said, softly enough, but Rachel could hear the steel in his voice, "don't get in between Abri and Trudi."

"Pa," Rachel called over Martin's shoulder, toward the store.

The Jew didn't frighten Martin but he slowly moved out of Rachel's way, holding her gaze.

Rachel was shaking when she walked into the store.

"What is the problem?" her father asked, coming out from behind the counter, a pair of scissors in his hand.

Rachel shook her head and hugged him.

The next day, Rachel walked down to Trudi's house.

Trudi didn't like the idea of taking soup to Abri. It wasn't that she hated him but she had a bad feeling about this. Her mother had always taught her that girls don't go into boy's bedrooms and boys didn't go into girl's bedrooms.

Her two best friends, Rachel and Cisca, sat in the kitchen at the table while she was busy cooking. No school today.

"I don't think this is a good idea," said Rachel, she didn't want to tell them what Martin had said.

Cisca nodded her agreement, "you don't even like him."

Trudi half turned toward them and put her hand on her hip, "it's not that I don't like him," she said, "there is just something about him. He is a bit creepy, don't you think"

"Well I think he has funny eyebrows," said Rachel. As a good Jewish girl, she knew she shouldn't speak bad of anybody but, secretly, she didn't like Abri at all.

"*Ag nou toe nou,*" retorted Trudi, "you are just looking for things now. My father has those same eyebrows."

She made the soup anyway. Now her mother and her father were telling her to take soup to Abri. What made Abri so special? She did make an excellent chicken soup and she was proud of it. When she took it off the stove, she went looking for Adrian to go with her. She would have felt more at ease if Adrian was with her but he was nowhere to be found

She wrapped the bowl in a kitchen towel, tied a knot in the top of the towel and walked up the road to Abri's house. Abri's housemaid, Johanna, opened the door to her and showed her into Abri's bedroom. Trudi was hoping that she would stay.

"Okay Johanna, you can go now," said Abri. He didn't sound very sick. He was fully dressed in his street clothes. He waited for Johanna to leave the room then patted the bed next to him.

"I will get you a tray and a spoon," said Trudi.

When she came back into the bedroom, Abri patted the bed again but she walked to the bedside table and put the soup down. She was starting to turn away when Abri reached out and grabbed her wrist. She tried to twist it away but Abri was too strong.

"I love you Trudi," he said with pleading in his voice, dragging her toward him onto the bed.

"Abri, this is not a good idea," Trudi pleaded with him, try to pull away.

She was much weaker than him, she twisted and pulled her body to the side.

"If you love me," Trudi was crying now, "ask my father if you can marry me but not this way Abri, it is wrong."

She tried to beat him off but he grabbed her wrists and pulled her underneath him.

She pleaded with all her heart now, "please Abri, please, she cried tearfully.

Abri tore at her pink dress and white petticoat, trying to get them up above her hips. The panty just tore apart. He had to hold her wrists with one hand while he fiddled with the buttons of his fly with the other. Trudi was bucking and heaving but that only served to excite him. He managed to force her legs apart with his knees. She clawed at his face, going for his eyes but he was too strong for her. She should have taken his eyes earlier but no use thinking of that now.

After that it only took a few seconds before it was all over. He had messed half of his load on the bed. Beside his strength, he wasn't much of a man. He threw himself sideways, panting. As he did up his fly, he saw there was blood on his bedspread.

"What's this!" he shouted, "Johanna!" he called.

Trudi scrambled to get her dress straightened before Johanna rushed in.

"Get this whore out of my bedroom!" he shouted, "she is trying to seduce me."

Johanna looked at the bed, at Trudi crying quite openly now and then at the blood and wet patch on the bedspread.

She helped Trudi up, "better you go quickly," she said softly to Trudi.

Trudi stumbled toward the door, still crying and still trying to straighten her dress. Her panty was left lying on the floor next to the bed. The few people in the street stared at her as she stumbled and ran home, still crying.

It had been so quick; she hadn't even taken her shoes off. She thanked God when she saw that her friends were still at her house. They rushed to meet her and helped her into her bedroom.

Trying to take breaths between sobs, Trudi told Rachel and Cisca what had happened. Rachel was furious but what could she, a Jewish woman, do. Then all three of them hugged each other and cried together. They helped Trudi clean up. It would take more than water to wash away the filth, physically and mentally. That is how Adrian found them, sitting on Trudi's bed together, sobbing and trying to comfort Trudi.

CHAPTER 6

Adrian had used his new revolver twice now. He didn't like killing but his commando had come across the raiders laying siege to *oom* Hannes' farm. They had the *oom* and the *tannie* holed up in the farm-house and it was only a matter of time until they would get up enough courage to charge, more than likely waiting for nightfall.

They were laying in a drainage ditch to the right of the house with a few young warriors circling toward the back in the bush. The flashes from the rifles gave their position away. Adrian's commando surprised the raiders and had them running. The battle was fast and furious. Adrian shot from the hip at point-blank range. *Oom* Hannes had downed two of them. The two big boerbull dogs lay dead in the front garden, both shot in the head but two warriors lay, their throats torn out, a few yards away.

Veldkornet Pieter called to the house to let oom Hannes know that they were coming in. The oom was laying in the front room and the tannie had her rifle at the back window in the kitchen. After composing themselves, both ushered the whole commando into the kitchen for *boerebiskuit,* rusks and coffee. Four men volunteered to stay at the farm-house until the next day. So, after saying goodbye and the Veldkornet giving thanks to God for their safety, they rode out.

While they rode, Adrian cleaned and reloaded his revolver. They rode fast. The Veldkornet wanted to reach home before nightfall.

Adrian was in high spirits as he left the commando and rode up the street to his home. Even as he unsaddled and wiped his horse down, he could faintly hear crying. As he went through the kitchen door, he could hear it coming from his sister's bedroom. It sounded like more than one person though.

He knocked on the door but no one answered so he opened and went in. The three girls were seated on the edge of the bed, Trudi between Rachel and Cisca. He knew Cisca as Francisca but Rachel and Francisca were both girls who he had grown up with. All three looked around at him and then cried even louder. At first, he thought that all of them had been injured. A bloody rag lay on the floor at their feet and Trudi's dress had blood stains across the front.

Cisca flew into his arms, "it's Trudi," she sobbed, "she's been raped."

"What?" he was devastated and came around to drop to his knees in front of her.

"Don't be angry with me," sobbed Trudi.

"Tsk," Adrian flipped his head, "don't' be silly. Who did this to you?"

"It was Abri," said Cisca, white faced.

"Bastard!" he exclaimed and stood up, starting to turn for the door.

"No, no!" exclaimed Trudi, "it's not for you to do anything. Tell our father, not Karl, I don't want Karl to know. Tell Johan."

Adrian stood collecting his thoughts. What Trudi said was true but it was hard for him to not immediately think of revenge.

"I am damaged now and everyone will know it. People saw me coming home. Johanna saw me, bloody on his bed."

Rachel and Cisca tried to console her. They put their arms around her, sitting on the edge of the bed. All three of them were sobbing again.

Adrian stormed out of the house, bumping into Truida coming in the front door.

"Oh hello, oops, where are you off to in such a hurry?" she asked, moving out of his way.

"Go see Trudi," Adrian said over his shoulder.

Truida's heart broke when she heard Trudi's story.

He pulled his horse around, mounting as it turned, not noticing Martin watching. Martin walked quickly down to Abri's house. He found Abri in the front room of his house.

"What happened?" asked Martin, "I saw Adrian in a big hurry."

"Coming here?" asked Abri wide eyed.

"No, the other way, maybe to Johan."

Then Abri told him the story of how Trudi had seduced him. Martin smiled wickedly. He didn't believe Abri in the least but it was a good story to tell. He wasn't expecting Abri to live much longer after Johan heard that his daughter had been raped. They would need a good story to protect Abri.

"Tell your mother the story, just as you told me," Martin said.

"I will," Abri said and he did.

In the meantime, Adrian had raced up to Johan's house. He threw the reins over the post in front of the stoep and stomped up the steps to the front door, his boots heavy on the stoep floor. Miriam met him at the door with a concerned look on her face but Adrian brushed her aside.

He turned on his heel in the front room, "where is he?" he almost shouted.

"If you are looking for me, here I am," said Johan, coming in from the kitchen.

Adrian turned to meet him.

CHAPTER 7

Johan was furious when he heard the news. He was raging. Adrian watched him with some satisfaction. He was sure that Trudi would get justice through Johan. Although it was true that no man would want damaged goods. Unless she moved away and hid the fact. Any man who had ever been with a woman would eventually find out though. Unless she married a virgin, who had never been with a woman. Women did have a knack of hiding the fact that they weren't virgins. None were clever enough to hide the fact from Adrian. He knew a handful in town who weren't virgins. He himself was no virgin.

Moving away may be the only option. Adrian thought he would speak to her about it. Before the scandal was noticeable. He left the revenge for Johan to sort out and rode back to his house.

Truida was hopping mad but she promised Trudi that she would not tell Karl, "You can live here as long as you like," she told the still tearful Trudi.

"The only way is for her to move and go live with our family in Pretoria," argued Adrian when they came back into the frontroom.

"You mean Karl's family," said Truida.

"I am sure that they will take her in," said Adrian.

"How do we ask them without telling Karl the whole story. And what if she falls pregnant"

"We will think of something."

"First we must think of Trudi," said Truida, "right now she wants to kill herself."

Johan's heart sank when he saw Truida come through the front gate. He knew why she was there. The servants had already told him their side of the story so he knew that the whole town knew already. Even Martin had been to see him. Now Martin was the son of Johan's cousin, so, as far as Johan was concerned, completely trustworthy. Johan was inclined to believe the servants though. They seemed very shocked and Johanna had almost been an eye-witness.

Martin told him the made-up story, of course, the story that he and Abri had agreed upon, so not so trustworthy.

"So, what are you going to do about this whole mess?" asked Truida when she was seated at the table in Johan's kitchen. She was spitting mad.

"I don't know, woman!" he retorted, "let me think clearly." He really didn't know what to do. He was torn between his love for his daughter Trudi and his son Abri. Although nobody, except

Jaqueline and Abri, knew that Abri was Johan's son.

"I will decide what to do," he said, sipping his coffee. He had his hands cupped around the mug so that Truida couldn't see his face and at that stage he really did mean to do something about it.

Truida glared at him, stood and marched out. He was expecting Jaqueline to come and pay him a visit too but instead Pieter came in.

"We have to ride now," he said with some urgency, The Bapedi are meeting with the Ndebele up north along the Drakensburg, "we must disperse them before they get organised. Word is that Mampuru is with them."

"Can you go?" asked Johan hopefully.

"No! People are going to start thinking that I am the Kommandant."

"Alright," said Johan reluctantly, "get the commando together and get them ready for a long ride. We will need supplies to last us for a few weeks."

In a way, Johan was a little relieved. It would delay him having to make a decision about Abri. He had been hoping to spend a bit of time with Helena while Uri was still away. Even though he knew that Abri was a bit slow, he did love him. How could a man not love his son, no matter what was wrong with him and no matter what he had done.

It had been raining but stopped while Johan was getting ready. He was bringing his saddle bag and bandolier over to where Phineas was saddling up for him when Adrian rode into the back yard. Adrian glared at him as he pulled his horse around. Ag, another son that he would have to deal with. Miriam ran out the kitchen door with his supplies. Phineas and Miriam stood together to wave to Johan as he rode out with Adrian by his side. The horses bunched their haunches and kicked up dust as they rode out.

They rode as far as the Steelpoort river before stopping for the night at a commando camp that had been there for more than a month. Uri, Helena's husband, was amongst the commandoes already there. They had been attacking the Bapedi across the river on and off for more than two weeks now.

Johan was not keen to look Uri in the eye. Luckily for him Uri was away on a patrol and wasn't expected back until the next afternoon. The men made ready to camp and gathered around the various camp-fires that were going with food cooking and coffee on the side.

Johan and Adrian found themselves at the same fire. There was a lot of talking and joking and news from home while meat and potatoes were passed around. The coffee flowed with the stories but the news of the rape hadn't reached them yet. It became late and the men slowly retired to their bed-roles, the last of them taking a last puff on their pipes. Johan didn't smoke and Adrian hadn't started yet.

After a-while, it was only Johan and Adrian left at the fire, facing each other.

Adrian poked the fire with a stick, "so, what are you going to do about Abri."

"Firstly, you must respect me and trust the decisions that I make," answered Johan.

Adrian was quiet for a bit, scratching in the fire, "I do love you but I now hate Abri. He raped your daughter, my sister. Doesn't that make you angry?"

"Yes, and he will receive his reward but I will decide what, when and where."

"He should be sent to prison in Pretoria, or worse."

"But not for you to say!" retorted Johan

Adrian grunted and scratched the coals. 'We will see about that' he thought to himself.

Johan scratched his beard, "I need to get this trimmed," he was thinking of Helena again.

"Do you know that an Italian opened shop next to the Jew?" Adrian asked, "he cuts hair, beard and head. He even shaves your face if you ask."

"I saw a shop like that in Pretoria," answered Johan, "ag, I will get Phineas to cut it again." He was glad that the subject was off Abri.

They spoke for a while of the river crossing. Luckily it wasn't rainy season so there were still a few places that they knew of where crossing wouldn't be too difficult.

The coals died to embers and they unrolled there bedding to the usual night sounds of the bush. They were always aware of the bush sounds. It was when those sounds changed that put them on the alert.

They woke before dawn but it was starting to lighten to their right when they drank their last coffee and swung into the saddle. The crossing that their Shangaan tracker chose was shallow, only touching their stirrups. After that it was a long hard ride. Johan stopped them short of the area where they expected to make first contact. Only a few hours ride would take them to the area where the scouts had last seen them. The sun was down to a finger above the horizon and Johan told them to make camp. Tomorrow would be a day to trust their destiny to God.

CHAPTER 8

One of the riders was an elder from their church and before they went to bed, he said a prayer for them. They would be outnumbered but they had better weapons now that they had their new Mausers. Most of their enemy only had muzzle loaders with a few rifles that they had captured. Johan knew that God preferred it that way so that they would be putting the outcome in his court. Helena was forgotten for the time being.

Before first light they were in the saddle again. Johan hoped to get as close as possible to the enemy before the sun came up. They wouldn't be able to hide their dust cloud in the early morning sunlight. The enemy would be alerted but wouldn't know what the dust cloud meant. It could just be a herd of buffalo.

The sun was just topping the trees when a tracker came back to Johan to say that there were about a thousand warriors over the next hill. Johan sent thirty men each under Pieter and Kobus, to the left and the right in the *koppies*. They would shoot down into the congregation and take out as many as possible before the enemy split and took cover. Johan knew enough to know the ways of the Pedi. They would split into groups and use pincer movements to counter-attack. Pieter and Kobus were to regroup with Johan in the centre for the main attack. Adrian stayed by Johan's side. He had wanted to go with Pieter but Johan stopped him.

The men were all excellent shots and the plan went well. Once they had regrouped, they rode to the west to attack from a different angle. The attack and counter-attack lasted all day with only one of the riders injured.

Lenni, the butcher, who some suspected had Jewish parents, operated to get the ball out of the wounded man's leg. Lenni knew how to part muscle with as little damage as possible.

The advantage that the commando had was the horses. At nightfall they could ride some distance away and make camp. It would take the Pedi half the night to get to their position so it was unlikely that they would follow. Johan's commando relaxed. They made cooking fires and sat around discussing the day's action.

Adrian waited until Johan was busy before calling two of the men he knew, aside. With the Shangaan tracker, under cover of darkness, they slipped across the Steelpoort river and walked their horses back to the battlefield. When they were opposite the Pedi camp they silently crossed back. The Pedi weren't expecting them so they didn't notice the blackened faces and chests of the white men with their shirts removed. They sat on the outskirts of the fires and listened for mention of the Pedi battle-plans.

Just after midnight, Adrian and his men slipped away again, across the river and back to their own camp. Johan was waiting for them when they arrived back.

"What they hell did you think you were doing? They could have caught you and tortured you to get information about us."

With that he turned and stormed back to his fire. Adrian had to admit that he had a point. He walked to where Johan was sitting with Pieter and Kobus.

"You are right," said Adrian and Johan looked up at him, "I am sorry. It was foolish but are you going to stay angry or do you want to hear what we found out?"

Johan beckoned him to sit, still looking angry.

This operation against the Bapedi lasted nearly six weeks. It could have lasted longer but the logistics of getting ammunition and food was just proving too much. The British had fought long campaigns against the Bapedi but they had the manpower and equipment that the Boers didn't have.

CHAPTER 9

Johan and his men arrived back home to cheers, praises and celebrations. Secretly, the women were just glad to have their men back home. Six weeks is a long time and much can happen in that time, as Johan was about to find out.

Firstly, Trudi had left on the wagon train that had come through from Delegoa Bay on its way to Pretoria. Truida had decided, with Karl's approval, that Trudi should go stay with her aunt in Pretoria where no-one knew of the rape. Not least of all with the fear that Trudi might fall pregnant. Adrian had queried the possibility. Also, the possibility that a child may be borne with a deformity. Could the pregnancy be aborted? But Truida had told him that with an abortion, the womb could get damaged and stop Trudi from ever having a child.

Anyway, Trudi had told Truida how Abri had messed on the bed but she knew that just one swimmer could do the job. The fact that Abri was Trudi's half -brother could mean that the child could be borne with a deformity.

So, amid much tears and nose wiping, as the Afrikaners say *snot en trane,* she climbed on a wagon one early morning with her suit-cases and waved goodbye to Truida, Rachel and Cisca. Both

Johan and Adrian were upset that they hadn't had a chance to say goodbye.

"I am holding you to your word," said Adrian to Johan when they were alone, "you must discipline Abri."

But Johan had other things to think about. He was wondering how he could get to see Helena again. Now that he was home, that ache in his heart came back. This was more than the feelings he had had for all the other women he had bedded. This time it was real love, he said to himself.

Sitting with Miriam and Phineas at breakfast he had hardly heard what they told him about what had been happening in Lydenberg these last few weeks. His mind was on Helena in everything that he did.

He was back three days when Miriam brought him a note. It was folded. Miriam walked out of the front room before he could open it.

It was only three words long and it didn't say who it was from. It simply said:

I AM PREGNANT

Johan's blood ran cold. He knew who it was from, definitely not Trudi. He felt nauseous and sat down on the couch. His mind raced, what? why? who? But, of course, he knew who it was and why and when. He sat for a while, bent forward with his head down, the note hanging from his fingers. What to do? He stood and walked to the kitchen where Miriam was working at the stove. She turned to look at him. Of course, she knew.

"Miriam," his voice didn't sound right, "ask miss Helena to please come to see me."

She nodded with pursed lips, turned and walked out. Johan walked back to the front room. He didn't sit down but stood in front of the fire-place, waiting.

He didn't have long to wait. Miriam brought Helena into the room. She looked beautiful, not dressed in white this time but in in a light blue dress. Neither women were smiling.

"Good-day Helena," Johan said, "please sit."

She sat, hands folded on her lap and looked up at him. Miriam left abruptly.

"Congratulations to you and Uri. How are you feeling?" He tried to sound cheerful.

"Uri has been gone for longer than three months," said Helena softly, "and the doctor said that I conceived six weeks ago."

Johan's blood ran cold again, "why did you even go to the doctor?"

"I wasn't expecting to fall pregnant and when I missed my period, twice now, I was worried. The doctor won't say anything to anybody but I am sure he can add the weeks"

Johan stood for a minute or two, staring into space. Finally, he said, "ok, I will think of something."

Helena stood and came to him and they put their arms around each other. Helena gave a little sob.

Johan kissed the top of her head, "don't worry, I will think of something."

"Do you love me?" she asked, looking up at his face.

"Yes," said Johan, without hesitation and kissed her forehead.

After she had left, Miriam came into the room. Johan was still standing staring into space. She stood quietly looking at him until his mind came back to the room.

"Call Phineas for me please," he said, his mind and body starting to function again.

He paced, deep in thought while Miriam went to call Phineas.

"Ah, Phineas," he said when Miriam brought him to the front room, "Please go find baas Pieter for me. I have something important to ask him."

After Phineas had left, Johan walked into the kitchen.

"Can I make the baas something to eat?" asked Miriam.

"Just coffee." He thought that he could do with something stronger to drink but he needed to keep a clear head.

Pieter soon came in. Johan was on his second cup. "Pieter," said Johan, "coffee?" he asked, standing up and shaking Pieter's hand.

Pieter nodded and Johan waved him to a chair.

"Miriam, coffee for baas Pieter please," Johan called, turning slightly toward the kitchen.

"Pieter," said Johan turning back and trying to put on a caring face, "I have been hearing about his man Uri."

"Oh, you mean Uri Burger?"

"Yes," answered Johan, "I hear that he has been away from home for a long time. Surely it's not right to keep him in the veld for so long?"

"Well, I have heard that he is a fearless fighter but I will find out how long he has been away."

"Yes," said Johan, "and I think you should bring him home for a while. Ask him to report to me. I would like to thank him."

"Of course."

They spoke about the situation with the Pedi a while longer, while Pieter finished his coffee, then he stood and left.

CHAPTER 10

Uri sat in a dip in the river-bank with his tracker, Kimile, at his side. Kimile, a Shangaan, was always at his side. He would have died for Uri without hesitation. Uri had saved Kimile's life when they were just young men. Kamile stood six foot six and was built like a brick. He also carried a Mauser with plenty of ammunition that he had taken off a dead Pedi.

Uri didn't shape up too badly himself and had the leadership qualities to go with it. He was a natural at the art of war and had thirty men that relied on him for leadership. Right now, his thoughts were on the enemy just ahead of him. He and Kimile were alone on the enemy side of the river. His men were on the far side of the river behind him, waiting for his signal.

Crocodiles were a big problem in the river but none had been seen here for a while. There was a lot of the usual noise from the bush but if they weren't careful, the bush would go silent when any animal or bird raised the alarm. It was uncanny the way the bush could go quiet in an instant This would alert the enemy to their presence.

The Pedi were settling down for the night. Kimile guessed there were about a hundred warriors.

Look-outs had been posted but they had been spotted by the pair. They would need to be pointed out to his men before the attack. If possible, the sentries would be taken out as a first step of the attack. Night was falling quickly now. Uri planned to surround the camp. He and Kimile had scouted the area and knew all the pitfalls and advantage points.

Kimile crept out of the dip and slipped into the river, much as a crocodile does, making as little noise as possible and listening for the tell-tale splash of a crocodile coming off the bank to join him. The water was cool to the bare skin but not cold. He didn't try to fight the current but swam diagonally across, allowing the current to take him a little downstream. Once on the other side, he crept through the bush toward where the men were waiting.

In the fading light he drew a map in the sand to relay Uri's battle plan to them. By the time the men entered the river, it was dark. There was a quarter moon, ideal for the situation. Uri watched from the other side of the river, looking for heads in the water. Happily, it was too dark. The men would land slightly downstream and then surround the camp.

Suddenly, Uri heard someone walking toward him from the camp. Uri hugged the side of the dip. The man saw the dip and veered off to the side, not at all trying to keep quiet. He wasn't expecting anyone on his side of the river. The man had come to urinate and was readying himself when Uri crept around behind him. Uri waited for him to start peeing. He stood up behind the man. Put his hand around, over his mouth and drove his knife down behind the left collar bone into his heart. The man spat into Uri's hand as he sank down in Uri's grasp, dead. So, one sentry gone. Kimile watched the men move into the river and glide slowly downstream. He would follow them to fight alongside Uri but he had done his job.

Long ago, Kimile had crossed the Limpopo River into the Transvaal from Mozambique when the girl he was courting had died of Maleria. The *sangoma*, witchdoctor, had given her the bark of a tree mixed in hot water, to drink but it hadn't helped. A white woman doctor had come and given her quinine but had said that it was too late. He had watched her shiver and shake with headaches so bad she couldn't lift her head. Toward the end she wouldn't eat and had finally died in his arms. Heartbroken, he had joined the wagon train coming up from Delegoa Bay bound for Pretoria. His plan was to look for work in Pretoria.

When the wagons stopped to replenish and spend the night in Kameelbult, he had met a fellow from Mozambique in the *shebeen*, beerhall, who had told him about Johan's commando. Johan was always looking for good trackers and scouts and the following day Kimile had joined Uri, a Veldkornet. They had bonded immediately and over the following months a friendship had developed in the heat of battle. The men in the commando trusted him with their lives.

Kimile slipped into the river behind the last man. When they reached the far bank, they spread out to encircle the camp. The plan went well and, with Uri's men attacking from all sides, the camp broke into confusion. Uri didn't want to kill them all and after only a few minutes of carnage, he broke off the attack. The ultimate objective was to stop the Pedi from attacking the farms. They had to learn that their attacks would bring retaliation and grief to them. Of course, the Pedi believed that the white man should not be there in the first place but they had to learn to co-exist. Of course, they never did. They had signed a treaty a few years back but as soon as the Pedi crowned a new king, the trouble started all over again.

Uri's men started slipping away into the dark bush and back to the river. Kimile had found Uri and the two of them entered the river together, still mindful of crocodiles. Luckily, no hippos had been spotted in this area for some time. Hippo's were more dangerous than crocodiles. The river was cool, not cold, I think you would call it refreshing. Not much had been said in words between them all night but they didn't need to.

The men were in good spirits when they rode into camp, some five miles east of the river. The cooks had a duiker stew ready and big pots of coffee. After cleaning up the men sat around a central fire to eat and drink coffee and then to light up their pipes with their feet up. Kimile didn't smoke a pipe. Tobacco hadn't been available in Mozambique. Men had brought small amounts back from the Transvaal when Kimile was growing up and it was becoming more popular there but difficult to get hold of. When the concertinas and guitars came out and the singing started, Kimile climbed into his bedroll and let the music put him to sleep.

The music was joyful in the evening but as the time went on it became melancholy. Uri sat and listened. The coffee was keeping him awake. He had drunk a splash of potato whiskey but didn't want to drink more. He knew what that could do to his senses and reactions in the morning. He was thinking of his wife, Helena, so beautiful. He loved her so much and planned to have lots of children with her when he had time to return to his farm. She was staying in their house in the village while he was away but as soon as he could, he would move with her back to the farm. He finally drifted off listening to the music and thinking of Helena.

Uri was up at first light, getting ready for the day. He loved being up early, when the bush was waking up. All the sounds of the birds and animals starting a new day. He had a plate of *pap* with milk and a cup of coffee and was starting to saddle up and get ready to ride when Pieter came riding into the camp. Pieter usually paid them a visit fairly often so it was no surprise. He waited for Pieter to join him and after greeting each other they went to sit under the fly tent where the planning usually took place.

"Uri," said Pieter seriously, "your courage has come to the attention of the commandant. Also, we have become aware that you haven't been home for several months. We want you to take a break, go home and see your wife for a few days, at least."

Uri didn't know what to think. He had such mixed feelings, proud that he had been noticed, not wanting to leave his men but also longing to see his wife.

Finally, he said, "I can't go now, *oom* Pieter. My men need me here."

"This wasn't a request," answered Pieter, kindly, "it is an order for your own good. When a man is too long in the veld he tends to start making mistakes. We don't want that to happen."

Uri looked down at the table.

Pieter carried on, "*oom* Johan wants to speak to you and thank you personally. You must ride back with us, you and Kimile."

Uri felt as if he was being torn in two. He wanted to ride with his commando but he knew he had to ride with Pieter. He walked back to the fire and told his men.

"We understand," said one of the men but Uri could see they were crestfallen.

"I will be back soon," said Uri, "I promise."

He packed his things and walked to where Kimile was holding the horses. They didn't speak but knew what each other was thinking. They waited in the shade of a tree for Pieter and his out-riders to finish their breakfast. Their horses had been rubbed down and watered and allowed to graze. Re-saddled, they mounted and were ready to ride.

The men stood and waved as the bunch pulled their horses around and kneed them into a canter. Pieter wanted to be home before dark. He was a bit disappointed in Johan. This wasn't the Johan he knew. The Johan he knew would have been happy to visit the men and even get involved in the fighting.

CHAPTER 11

Johan was waiting impatiently at home. If Uri stayed the night with his wife, everyone would think that he had made Helena pregnant. Miriam knew of course, but she was very loyal to Johan. Even though she was disgusted with him, she wouldn't say a word.

Eventually Pieter arrived with Uri. The whole delegation crowded into Johan's front room (lounge). They were a bit sweaty from the day's long ride but no one minded even though, to Johan, the stink of sweaty bodies was ripe. Uri came to stand in front of Johan. In his heart Johan knew that he was only doing this for show but he went ahead anyway.

"Uri," he said, "We are very proud of you. It has come to our attention that you have been a fearless fighter and have been out fighting for your fellow men for several months now."

"Three months now, *Oom*." Uri answered, with his hat held screwed in a roll behind him.

"Yes," Johan went on, "and for this we want to say that your whole nation is thankful to you and want you to have a few days' rest. In fact, take all the time you like to visit with your wife, before even thinking of going back to the commando."

The crowd in the room cheered and most of them stepped forward to pat him on the back. Uri felt embarrassed. He didn't feel that he deserved all this attention. He was just doing his duty.

The crowd filed out and Uri followed them. It was starting to get dark outside as Johan watched them file out the gate. He was starting to relax. Things were working out. Uri would surely sleep in his wife's bed that night and all of Johan's worries would be over. He turned to the kitchen where Miriam had cooked him a delicious supper of lamb stew and milk tart to end it.

Johan took his time eating. He sat alone. Miriam didn't join him as she usually did, she only bustled in to serve his pudding of milk tart and pour his coffee. Johan didn't ask her why, he knew already. Sipping his second cup, he thought about how things would be after the baby was born. It wouldn't be the first time that he had watched his off-spring born with another father standing by. He poured himself a short glass of brandy, especially brought up from the Cape and he savoured the burning gold liquid roll down his throat.

Finally, he went to bed but, for some reason he couldn't sleep. He fought the urge to go make sure that his plan was working. He didn't know why he would think that it wouldn't. It was after midnight before he fell asleep but still woke up at the usual time, just after daybreak. He had thought that he had heard a noise on his front stoop the night before so he stumbled out to have a look but, nothing. In the kitchen he cleared the ash in the stove and loaded wood into the grate.

By the time Miriam came in, the fire in the stove was blazing nicely and the water was just boiling. Miriam was surprised to see him in the kitchen before her but didn't say anything.

"Morning Miriam," said Johan cheerfully. Despite the fact that he had not slept well, he felt cheerful this morning.

Miriam grunted. She was still trying to get over her disgust at what he had done. It wasn't that she was jealous of Helena. She knew that their cultural differences would never allow her to be with Johan. There were a few in her community, she knew, who had crossed that line, more out of lust than love but it always came to nothing.

"I am glad that *baas* Uri is having a chance to be with his wife for a few days," Johan continued.

Miriam just grunted again as she poured his coffee. She was having difficulty speaking to him.

Johan sat in silence while Miriam made the porridge. It wasn't long before Phineas came in.

"Morning Phineas," Johan repeated, "I am glad that *baas* Uri can have a few days with his wife."

Phineas sat down at the table and waited for Miriam to pour his coffee before replying, "no," he said, "*baas* Uri slept on your stoop last night and left at first light for the commando."

Johan thought he was going to throw up. He gripped the table and had to take a few minutes to calm himself.

"Why?"

"I don't know," replied Phineas.

Miriam smiled to herself and stayed facing the stove.

"As soon as you are finished eating, go call baas Pieter," said Johan.

"*Baas* Pieter has also left for the commando," said Phineas.

"And baas Kobus?"

"Yes, I will call him," said Phineas.

Johan was beside himself. This was very bad news. It felt like ages before Kobus finally came in. He was very cheerful, which upset Johan even further.

"Why did Uri go back to the commando?" Johan asked him, trying to stay calm. "Uri needed to rest. Mistakes are made when men are in action too long."

"We tried to persuade Uri to stay," answered Kobus, "but he said that he couldn't rest while his men were under the sky and needed him."

"Bring him back here. I fear that if he stays in battle too long, he will be killed."

"It's not going to help, bringing him back here again. He won't stay," insisted Kobus.

"He must come back," said Johan, "he is going to kill himself if he stays there. Tiredness is going to kill him,"

"What can I say to him to make him come back?"

"Tell him that I want to give him a medal," said Johan, "and a party."

CHAPTER 12

Kobus was puzzled, why this insistence. He did agree though that Uri deserved a medal. He left right away for the battle-front. Arriving at the camp late that night, he found Uri sleeping already. Kobus shook the bed-role with his foot. Uri came out with his Mauser in his hand. He was working the bolt when he saw Kobus standing in front of him.

"*Oom* Kobus," he greeted him.

Kobus nodded to him, "You need to go back to Kameelbult," he said, "Johan wants to honour you for your good work here in the field. He wants to hold a party in your honour and give you a medal. He also wants you to get a break from the fighting."

"That is not at all necessary."

"That is not for you to say," countered Kobus, "and I agree with him that you must take even a short break now. You must leave at daybreak."

Uri struggled to sleep for the rest of the night but early the next morning, after talking to Kimile, he rode for Kameelbult again. The guinie-fowl along the way will start recognising me if this carries on, he thought. His head was full of thoughts as he rode. And such mixed feelings. He waved to friends as he rode into town.

Johan met him on the stoop, "go home, get cleaned up and rest a bit," he said. Tonight, I want to have a big *braai* in your honour and to give you a medal. You may bring your wife with you too."

After washing, Uri was so tired, he just flopped down on his bed and went to sleep. Helena had to wake him to get ready for the braai. When Uri walked into Johan's yard with Helena on his arm, all the well-known towns people were already there. They shouted his name and clapped him on the back. He felt a bit embarrassed. He didn't think that he deserved all this attention.

Johan buzzed around him, plying him with whisky but Uri knew how to go with the flow here. When no one was looking he poured the whiskey out and filled his glass with water. He couldn't understand why Helena didn't want to drink any alcohol. She said that it was because of an upset stomach. Anyway, women were funny that way.

Drums were rolled and he was presented with his medal. Plenty of meat was eaten and whiskey drunk all round and finally Uri and Helena left for home.

CHAPTER 13

Johan watched them leave. He had given Uri enough whisky to sink a ship but Uri still seemed to be fairly steady on his feet. Uri was swaying a bit on his feet. He didn't want to put on too much of an act. Johan turned back to the fires. He was pleased with the way the evening had played out. Surely now Uri would sleep with his wife. Anyway, the whole town had seen how Uri had left with his wife, clearly under the weather.

Johan had a sleepless night. He couldn't understand why but he felt slightly jealous of Uri right now. Just knowing that Helena was laying naked in her bed with Uri made Johan wonder if he had done the right thing. Johan slid out of bed and went to stand at the window. He couldn't see Helena's house from there but at least there was a cool draught blowing into the room. Finally sleep came to rescue him but it was a disturbed sleep. Almost as if a little demon was bugging him, which it definitely was.

Johan was up early. He walked down to the water trough, peering to see if he could see any movement from the Burger's house. Strange, he thought, he couldn't see any sign of Uri's horse. Oh well, it could be tethered out of view. He pulled his boots on and selected a clean shirt.

Breakfast was a cheerful matter. He chatted to Miriam and Phineas, purposefully keeping away from the subject of Uri and Helena. He was on his second cup of coffee when Kobus knocked at the kitchen door.

"Come!" called Johan cheerfully.

Kobus came in, taking his hat off, "are you returning with me to the commando."

"Yes of course," answered Johan, waving Kobus into a chair and signalling to Miriam for coffee to be poured, "and call Uri to join us for the ride," he added.

"Uri left for the commando last night," answered Kobus, "as soon as he left the *braai*."

"What!" Johan jumped out of his chair.

"Yes," said Kobus, "we tried to talk him out of it but he wouldn't be persuaded. He said he had to get back to his men. He said that he couldn't sleep in a bed while his men slept on the ground."

Johan forced himself to calm down. He started pacing, "I told him to spend the night with his wife."

Kobus shrugged and grunted. Miriam and Phineas glanced at each other.

Johan paced again. He needed another plan and the devil was there to provide him with one.

"Anyway," said Johan and made as if he was dismissing the subject of Uri, "I think I must join the commando again. I will be there by nightfall."

Kobus left and Johan made ready to ride. When he walked out where Phineas was holding his horse, Miriam ran out of the kitchen with a small bag of *padkoss*, food for the road.

Miriam and Phineas stood together, watching Johan ride out and down the street.

"This is not going to end well," said Miriam.

"Not for Uri," agreed Phineas.

"Not for anyone," said Miriam, turning and walking back into the house.

CHAPTER 14

Johan did reach the camp as the sun was setting over the hilltops to the west. The men cheered when he rode in. Pieter grabbed his reins as Johan stepped down.

"Good to see you," said Pieter, as they walked to the fly-tent.

"What is the problem here," asked Johan, sitting down at the table, "all we have to do is drive them back into the mountains and then just make sure that they stay there. Once we have them in the mountains, it should only take a few men to keep them there."

"The problem is," answered Pieter, "when we get them into the mountains, they are very good at ambushing us from the rocks and crags. We have lost some good men up there."

Johan's plan was taking shape in his head, "tomorrow morning, at first light, take all of your men to the south side of their encampment and push them toward the mountains. Once you have them there, draw back and put your best men to harass them out of their hiding places. Let Uri lead these men. He is a man who can get the job done."

"That is going to be dangerous."

Pieter didn't like the plan but Johan was right. They had too many men in the field. The men needed to be at home, working their farms, not spending their lives on commando.

Pieter nodded, "but are you sure it is wise to let Uri lead these men, you said yourself that he is becoming battle weary?"

"Yes!" answered Johan adamantly, "I want him there. He is the best man for the task."

Pieter turned and walked out, calling one of the sentries to him, "call all the veldkornets and their seconds here to the command tent."

Johan stood by while Pieter addressed the men. They argued amongst themselves. Not all of them liked the idea. They knew how dangerous it was for them once they got up into the mountains. The Pedi were very good at hiding and attacking from the high rocks and crags. Finally, they settled down and Pieter went into detail. He would leave the picking of men to the veldkornets except for Uri. He would speak to Uri himself. Johan did speak to Uri. He made it sound as if he was bestowing a great honour on Uri, sending him and his men ahead into the mountains.

When they assembled together at daybreak, Johan was a bit startled to see Adrian among the men.

He shouldn't have been surprised, he knew that Adrian joined the commando on and off when he wasn't doing something for his step-father.

It reminded Johan that he hadn't done anything about Abri yet and knew, when Adrian stared at him, that he was thinking the same thing. He turned his attention back to the task at hand but promised himself that he would attend to Abri when he returned home, although he still didn't know what he was going to do. He loved Trudi but also loved Abri as he loved Adrian.

"I want Adrian by my side today," said Johan to Pieter, "I need him to relay any messages."

Pieter nodded and beckoned to Adrian as the men mounted. When they entered the river, Adrian was with Johan but the two men didn't make eye contact. All the men were out of the water before they were seen by the enemy sentries. The first contact was furious and Johan saw two of his men go down before the Pedi started drawing back to the foot-hills. Johan allowed the battle to move forward but motioned Adrian to him and rode to make sure that the wounded men were being taken care of. It was only when he was satisfied, that he joined the drive.

The Pedi fought a brave defensive withdrawal but they were no match for the accuracy of the Boer marksmen. Pieter wouldn't let Johan go to the front of the battle. He always maintained that

Johan's military knowledge was too important to put in harm's way unnecessarily. Even so, Johan heard bullets buzz very close to his head. The zip and then thud as the bullets wacked the trees.

As they reached the foothills, Johan called Adrian to his side, he shouted above the noise, "go tell *oom* Pieter to send the strike forward. He will know what I mean!"

Adrian nodded and kneed his horse forward. Through the dust, Johan saw Adrian pass on the message. He saw Pieter shout to one of his men and the man push his horse to Uri's position, fighting on the flank. The whole commando still moved forward but Uri and his men were now in front. Uri seemed to have a charmed life. Through the foothills the battle raged and Johan saw more of his men go down but Uri was still in front with his tracker by his side.

The mountains loomed now and the Pedi started disappearing into the terrain that they knew so well, the *Drakensberge* or Dragon Mountains. Also known as The Barrier of Spears. Uri and his men pushed forward with Kimile ever by his side. Out of his original thirty men, Uri only saw ten strung out behind him. Uri wondered about this. Surely he couldn't have lost twenty men? He didn't know that Pieter had told all of his men, except him, to not take chances once they came into the mountains.

When Uri next looked behind him, he only saw Kimile. Uri and Kimile both now rode with their feet out of the stirrups, ready to drop off the back of their horse in an ambush. The large rocks were close to the sides of the trail now. A warrior could easily drop off a rock above them, onto their back. The trail still led upward. Soon Uri himself would fall back.

As he was about to do so, he thought he saw movement around the corner of a rock. He signalled Kimile to dismount. Uri looked beyond Kimile but couldn't see any of his men following along behind them. They trailed the reins of their horses and crept forward, thick dust beneath their feet, hugging the side of a massive rock that stretched up into the sky, crags and small bushes jutting out. Uri scanned the trail surface to check for sign but there were no clear footprints in the dust. They held their Mausers at the ready. Uri pushed his hat off his head so that he had a clearer peripheral vision.

CHAPTER 15

Around the corner from Uri and Kimile, Kiewiet the Pedi pushed his back against the rock. He had been practicing all his adult life for such a moment, ever since he had turned twelve and left his grandmother's side to be with his father. His father had taught him the way of the spear.

He held a spear in each hand. As yet, he hadn't been able to get his hands on a rifle. Since he had joined the ring of warriors, they had never advanced over dead Boers but both spears now were wet with blood. He had come close enough to cause damage. This would be the moment when he would earn the respect of the other warriors and be a tribute to his father's death.

He slid against the rock to get into the right position, held his left spear directly above the right. He steeled himself to stand steady as the white man came around the corner. To wait for the black man to follow. It was only a split second but felt like ages. The spear left his right hand in a blur of motion. The left spear dropped to his right hand. He whipped his hip for momentum.

The white man was falling, the blade of the spear spurting blood out his back, the shaft protruding from the chest. The second spear was on its way, as the black man lifted his rifle that small distance to take aim. The rifle thundered in that narrow pass, almost deafening Kiewiet. As the mist descended before his eyes, he saw his spear blade pass through the black man's neck. The black man had tried to move out of the way but he had been concentrating on the shot. A split second too late.

Kimile died knowing that he hadn't been able to save his *N'kosi*. As his knees hit the ground and the mist descended, he saw Uri laying on the ground in front of him, his rifle flung to the side. Uri had heard the shot behind him and had seen the Pedi fall, the red badge of courage blossom on his chest above the heart.

Uri now lay in the dust. He could feel his body growing cold as his blood flowed freely into that dust. He thought of Helena and saw her standing in front of him but she seemed to be holding a baby. Then his face was on the cool sand. He wanted to sleep. He felt no pain, only a longing in his heart for Helena. Someone was turning him over. He heard a voice. Someone was calling his name, trying to talk to him. Then he was walking down a long tunnel of light, Kimile by his side. Somehow, he knew, their fighting days were over.

When Kobus felt for a pulse on Uri's neck, there was nothing. Kobus had watched Uri's eyes grow blank. It was strange, the way a man's life left him. This wasn't the first time that Kobus had watched this happen but this time it felt more personal. He couldn't understand why Pieter had pulled the men back and allowed Uri to go forward. He didn't know if, maybe, Uri just hadn't listened to the command. That would be like Uri to push forward regardless.

Kobus' men had silently followed him up the pass. Kobus and his men lifted Uri and Kimile and carried them down to the horses. They lay them across their saddles and mounted. Kobus had seen the young Pedi laying dead not far away but knew that his people would fetch him as soon as they knew it was safe to do so, a warrior indeed.

The light was leaving the day by the time the men rode into camp. Kobus and Pieter walked up to the fly-tent where Johan was waiting for them.

"We have pushed them back into the mountains," said Pieter. "They lost a lot of men. I don't think they will be back for a long time."

"And our men?" asked Johan. He could see from their demeanour that his plan had worked.

"We lost four men," answered Pieter, "including the tracker, Kimile, about a dozen wounded, some badly but not life threatening."

"The names of the dead?"

"Uri, Kimile, Piet du Toit and his brother, Tinus."

"Are you sure they are dead?" Johan pressed him, feigning concern.

"Kobus was there when Uri died," answered Pieter, "and we have brought all their bodies back for a decent burial.

"We warned the men to be careful and not go too far into the mountains," said Kobus, "but Uri just kept on going."

"Don't feel too bad," said Johan, "you did warn them and what is done, is done."

Inside, Johan was elated. He slept like a baby that night, even though it was on the ground. He would have to wait to show a decent mourning period before even visiting Helena again. Not too long though, otherwise the lump would be showing. He tried to seem nonchalant about packing up and going home, even trying to show that he was mourning the loss of his men. Things had worked out exactly as he had hoped.

They left at first light and the going was slow with the dead bodies in a wagon. All the way home he was planning his next move and it felt to him as if he was riding on clouds. Adrian rode beside him and was trying to talk to him but Johan was in no mood for small-talk. For Adrian, it wasn't small talk, it was serious. Riding into his yard, for Johan, handing the reins to Phineas and walking into the kitchen felt like a dream.

Miriam welcomed him back. She was always pleased to see that he had survived. She didn't yet know about Uri. Phineas came in to tell her what he had heard and she then took Johan's wistfulness as sadness at the death of Uri. She felt sorry for Johan then and started making his favourite rabbit and pork pie.

Helena was genuinely shocked and sorry to hear of the death of Uri. She didn't know about Johan's plotting behind the scenes. She immediately started wearing black and veiled her face, as was appropriate. A long black dress with black stockings, in case her ankles showed and a black *cappie,* hat. Also, black gloves, when she went into the street.

Even in black, Johan thought she was beautiful. His heart ached for her and he walked around like a school-boy in love. Not eating all his food and forgetting to do things. Miriam wondered how long this mourning would go on. Maybe it was for all his men who died, that he was mourning.

The next month felt like a year. He couldn't eat properly; he couldn't sleep properly. Finally, the time came when he thought the mourning time was over. Well, he couldn't wait any longer. He noticed that Helena was wearing looser clothes. Hopefully the townspeople thought that she was putting on a bit of weight.

He went to visit her one afternoon and, in front of her maid, he proposed to her on his knee. The Jew had found a ring all the way from Holland. The diamond had been found in a river in Lightenburg and shipped to Holland to be made into a beautiful ring. The wedding took place only a few weeks later, with Helena already looking very plump. Of course, she immediately moved into Johan's house.

CHAPTER 16

Ciska and Rachel stood at the wagon station. The wagon train was due in from Pretoria on its way to Delegoa Bay. Time had passed and the gossip surrounding Trudi's rape had died down. Adrian had been in touch with Trudi and had told her to come home. Karl and Truida were also at the wagon station, seated in the office. Well, it was just a room in a house that had been turned into a waiting room for merchants waiting for goods being brought in, either from Pretoria or Delegoa Bay.

Coffee was being served, of course, to the merchants waiting there. Merchant's wagons were standing by to one side. The place was bustling, so nobody noticed the two girls standing in the shade of a Jacaranda tree. Even Rachel's father didn't notice them standing there. The Jew was waiting for some particularly beautiful material that he had ordered from France. He sat beside the baker, one of his few friends.

"Why isn't Adrian here to meet her?" asked Ciska, not taking her eyes of the dirt road ahead of them.

"He may be on commando," answered Rachel, looking around for him. Just the sound of his name made her neck heat up under the high collared dress.

Both girls were excited to be seeing their friend again but also slightly apprehensive. They weren't sure what Abri's reaction would be if he heard that Trudi was home. Abri had left school, not going back after the rape. He had told everyone that Trudi had seduced him. Some people even believed him. After all, he was easily influenced. He had become a loud pompous layabout with friends of the same calibre.

Cisca and Rachel were hopeful that they would get Trudi back home without too many people noticing. Dust of the approaching wagons had been seen for a while now and men, waiting for their goods, were slowly coming forward, peering into the distance, along the winding road. It was always exciting when new, fresh goods arrived. Especially the clothes and material for the ladies that would be unpacked in the Jew's shop that night, ready for display the next day.

At last the wagons came into view and the cracking of whips could be heard as the oxen rumbled the wagons forward through the dust. They had made good time. Leading the train was a covered wagon with a few passengers, trying to look dignified but still covered with dust kicked up by the oxen. Half hidden amongst them was Trudi.

Cisca and Rachel struggled to contain themselves. As Trudi climbed down, both girls instinctively glanced at Trudi's midriff and, secretly, breathed a sigh of relief to see that she was as flat as a board.

Karl had a buggy waiting and, after lots of hugs and kisses, Trudi headed for home. Cisca and Rachel would give Trudi a few hours to settle in and freshen up before visiting her, although the three of them were bursting to be together. Rachel came in close to give Trudi a hug. She placed the palm of her hand against Trudi's abdomen and looked her in the eye. Trudi shook her head as the message passed between them. When they broke apart, both were smiling.

Adrian was there but he kept out of sight. It had been his idea that Trudi come back home and Truida had agreed with him. His aunt had sent Truida a note to say that Trudi was definitely not pregnant. Adrian was overjoyed to see his sister but kept out of sight, keeping a watchful eye for Abri. He would have loved to see Abri start something so that he could finish it. Abri didn't show.

Adrian wasn't really sure that Abri even knew that Trudi was back. He hoped not. Adrian had seen the two girls send a message when they hugged but he already knew.

It was late afternoon by the time Adrian knocked on Trudi's door. She rushed into his arms when he walked in. Cisca and Rachel were there, sitting on the edge of the bed. Rachel wished she could rush into his arms but she just stared at the floor.

"It's good to be home," said Trudi, tearfully.

"I am glad to have you home," answered Adrian, "you will be safe here."

"Safe but tarnished," said Trudi, still full of tears, "I will have to leave again one day if I want to lead a normal life. Aunt Sharon says that I am always welcome in the Barron's home."

"We don't need to talk about that now," said Adrian as Trudi walked back to the bed to sit, once again, between the two girls.

"They tell me that still nothing has been done about Abri," Trudi half turned to the girls on the bed, "is that true?"

Adrian could feel his anger welling up, "yes, it is true but our father has been busy with the marauding Pedi so maybe we should give him a chance. He has also taken a new wife."

Trudi was surprised, "who?"

"The widow Burger," answered Adrian, "her husband, Uri, was killed in battle a little while back. Let's see what he does in the next few months. After that, I may be forced to do something."

Trudi sat quietly with the girls on the bed and Adrian left them to do what girls do. He was starting to fancy Rachel. She looked radiant but the nightmare was that she was Jewish and everyone in town knew that she was Jewish. Him visiting her would never be accepted. And he was not Jewish. Would she even consider him as a suitor? He didn't think her father would. He knew from Johan that the Jew only associated socially with other Jews. Adrian didn't understand why.

Adrian had many things worrying him at that moment. Rachel had never even spoken to him except once when they had been put together in school class to study a frog and that was only because she was scared out of her wits about touching the frog. She had clutched his arm and it was as if an electric shock had run through him.

Even before that, when waiting in front of the school. Adrian had his back to a wall and Rachel was standing a short distance in front of him, a wagon had come past pulled by two oxen. The wagon had come close to them and Rachel had stepped back, stumbling against him. Their bodies had touched as he had steadied her with his hands on her elbows. She had glanced back over her shoulder and their eyes had met. Still young teenagers really but the spark was there.

He glanced back as he left the room but Rachel was hard in discussion with Trudi.

CHAPTER 17

Johan thought he was the happiest man on earth. Helena was now married to him. The love of his life. Well, that is the way he thought at the time. She was heavy with child now. From the way the baby was situated in her belly, the old birth-mothers reckoned it was going to be a boy.

Adrian came to see Johan about Abri but he couldn't be bothered with all that right now. Helena was absolutely glowing and, as her time to give birth grew closer, he loved her and the unborn child more than he loved himself, and that was saying something. Even Miriam couldn't help getting into the mood of the coming birth. He didn't think that Miriam would ever forgive him but at least she was putting sugar in his coffee again.

When he and Helena had been leaving the church on Sunday, the *dominee* had shaken his hand at the door but then had said that he wanted to speak to him sometime. Someone had then started speaking to the *dominee*, so Johan had walked away. Johan knew that he should go see him but the right time just hadn't presented itself. Anyway, he could guess what the *dominee* was going to say to him.

The time came. The doctor and a *vroedvrou*, midwife, were in the bedroom and every few minutes Helena screamed to raise the roof. Miriam was rushing in and out with a basin of hot water and towels. This wasn't the first birth that Johan had sat through but in many respects, it was the most important. The screaming and rushing around carried on all day. It was Helena's first child and she was having a hard time.

It had started at daybreak when Helena's water broke and Johan had rushed to call Miriam. That is when all the rushing around had started and at about eight, Helena's screaming had started. He had never heard such anger from her before. She had ordered him out of the bedroom. Then the doctor and midwife had arrived and after that he could have just been a piece of furniture in the front room for all the attention he was getting. He even had to go make his own coffee.

At last the screaming stopped. It was getting dark outside. Johan heard the cry of a baby and knew that it was all over. Miriam was lighting the lamps in the house when the midwife came out of the bedroom and told Johan that he could go in. Helena was holding the baby wrapped in cloths.

She beamed up at Johan, "it's a boy," she said softly.

Johan felt as if his heart would burst. He peered at the little screwed-up face and held Helena's hand.

The doctor was washing up in the basin and, as he dried his hands, he motioned for Johan to follow him out.

"Everything went well," he said, "despite the baby lying feet down."

Johan could hardly contain himself. He was trying to act like a leader but he was acting more like a first-time father. Everything else faded in his mind. It is doubtful whether he even considered thanking his God. So, it was a bit of a shock or not really shock but maybe puzzling, when the *dominee,* pulled him to the side after church the next morning. He led Johan around the side of the church and waited until nobody was within earshot.

"Johan, I asked you to come see me," he said, a little sternly.

Johan wasn't too happy with being spoken to in this tone of voice, "I have been busy *Dominee.*"

The *dominee* dismissed this with a wave of the hand, "*Siener* Prophet Esterhuis had told me that he wants to bring a case before you. He says that it is very important."

That rattled Johan. The *siener* was not someone to be taken lightly. Everyone believed that God had given him a gift of seeing into the future, of prophesying.

"I am really sorry *Dominee*. I didn't realize. I thought that you only wanted to discuss something with me."

The *dominee* grunted, "not important then?"

Johan felt a little cold sweat break out on his skin, "please tell him that I will see him any time at his convenience."

The *dominee* nodded and turned to walk back to the front of the church. Johan was there alone that Sunday. Helena was at home with her new-born baby. He waited to calm himself before following the *dominee*. It was strange how the old prophet commanded such respect. Maybe not so strange because everyone believed that he received the voice of God. Johan went home feeling apprehensive. Helena was also apprehensive.

CHAPTER 18

It wasn't many days after that, that the prophet came to visit. It was early morning, just after breakfast. He smiled to put Johan at ease as he walked into the front room. He was dressed very ordinary, as far as Johan was concerned. Short beard and short hair. He didn't know what he was expecting. Helena was there holding the baby, standing in front of the fireplace.

"*More, Siener,*" she greeted him respectfully.

"*More* Helena. I would like to speak to Johan about a private matter please." He moved to a chair in the corner but didn't sit down,

"Of course," she answered and walked out.

Johan motioned the prophet to sit down and sat down facing him.

The prophet sat but then leant forward to speak, "Johan, I have a case that I need your opinion on."

"Of course," Johan said, "go ahead."

"Well, the problem is this," said the prophet, "a poor man in the township had a lamb that he cherished. It was the only one he had. From its birth, he had cherished it, so much so that it slept on the foot of his bed. He called it by name."

Johan nodded, listening intently.

"Now, a rich man here in town had an important visitor come to stay. This was a man who could bring important trade to the town. The rich man, who had many sheep and lambs, didn't want to slaughter his own stock. He took the poor man's lamb and handed it to the butcher for slaughter. Our butcher, unknowingly, slaughtered it and dressed it for the rich man and delivered it to his house on the evening that the visitor arrived."

Johan was upset by the story. "Do you need me to tell you that I think that the rich should be punished?"

"It doesn't end there," the prophet carried on, "because the rich man thought that the poor man may make trouble for him, so he had the poor man murdered."

"This man should be hanged!" exclaimed Johan, jumping up, "do you know who this man is and where we may find him?"

"The man is you," said the prophet softly.

Johan nearly fell over with shock, "what do you mean? I never stole anyone's lamb nor had anyone murdered."

"You did," said the prophet, standing to face Johan. He stood eye to eye with him. "You know what I am referring to. The Lord your God is angry for what you have done."

Johan felt weak and steadied himself with a hand on the mantlepiece. After a few minutes, he turned back to the prophet, "what needs to be done?" he asked him.

The prophet searched for Johan's eyes, "you will not die but you must ask forgiveness."

"And Helena?" Johan asked.

"Helena will not die," answered the prophet.

Johan knew what was coming next.

"Your son will not see his first birthday."

Johan felt his heart melt, "rather punish me," protested Johan. He was fearful of touching the prophet but held his hands together as if in prayer.

"This is your punishment; your actions will always have consequences." said the prophet. He picked up his hat, half bowed to Johan and walked out the front door.

What was he going to say to Helena? Thought Johan, but he didn't need to. He heard a keening sound coming from the kitchen. Helena must have been listening to the conversation.

When Johan walked into the kitchen, Helena and Miriam were holding each other and sobbing.

CHAPTER 19

Miriam shuffled out of the kitchen as Helena came into Johan's arms. Johan couldn't help sobbing too. Johan looked over to the baby lying in his cradle. After a few minutes the sobbing subsided. The two of them went to the cradle and, holding hands, knelt down next to it. Johan didn't know what to say to God except to ask forgiveness. Surely God would forgive them. He stood, kissed the top of Helena's head and left.

He walked down to the water trough, took off his shirt and washed. Then he went in and dressed in black.

He walked through the kitchen, "I'm going to visit the *dominee*," he said to Helena.

Helena nodded and made a small sound of agreement. She pushed her hair back and wiped tears away as Johan kissed her.

Johan wondered if the *dominee* would even be at his house but he was.

"Let's go into the church," he said when he saw Johan.

"*Dominee,*" he said when they sat down in the pews that Johan had helped pay for, "I need you to pray for us," and he told him what the prophet had said. "How do we even know that what he said will happen?"

"We can read in the bible, in Paul's letter to the Ephesians, that some men or women will have the gift of being able to prophesy. This man has been tested and proven to have that gift."

"Will you pray for us?" Johan asked.

"God is not going to listen to me above you," answered the *dominee,* "we are all equal in God's eyes but I will pray with you."

So, they prayed. Johan beseeched God, prostrating himself on the floor of the church. The *dominee* knelt and prayed.

It was getting dark when Johan finally went home. He shaved off his beard and didn't eat, only drinking water. He slept outside the house on the ground and dressed in the same black clothes every day. He didn't even bother to wash himself. Miriam and Phineas tried to persuade him to eat and Pieter came to see him. Pieter thought that Johan was ill with some stomach disease that was going around.

After a time, the baby fell ill. The doctor came to see the child but couldn't find what was wrong with him but gave him a tonic that had seemed to be helping the other people in the town with this stomach bug. No matter what they tried, the baby became worse by the day. Johan and Helena spent their nights on their knees, praying beside the cradle.

Johan in desperation, even thought of trying to sacrifice some animal but the *dominee's* words rang like a death bell in his mind, "God wants your hearts, not your sacrifices." The baby became worse until, after seven days, the baby died.

"How are we going to tell him that his son died," the doctor asked the nurse. Miriam was standing with them.

"He is taking this so badly," said Miriam, "he might kill himself."

Johan and Helena cried all night and, after a service in the church, the *dominee* buried the baby in the graveyard on the hill. The whole household was grief-stricken. Pieter and Kobus brought their wives around to pay their respects. Adrian and Trudi came with Truida and Karl. Even the Jew and his daughter came to pay their respects.

The day after the funeral, Johan washed and dressed in fresh clothes. He ate slowly to get his strength back. Miriam and Phineas couldn't understand why he was acting this way after the death of his son.

"What is this?" Miriam dared to ask him, "while the child was alive you fasted and wept and prayed continuously at his bedside. Now that he is dead, you wash and eat. Don't you mourn?"

"While he was alive, I tried everything that I could think of to show that I was sorry for my sins but now that he is dead, I can do nothing to change that. I couldn't persuade God. I can't bring him back from the dead. I will go to him but he won't come back to me." Johan felt that his spirit was broken.

The prophet hadn't come to see them before the funeral but the evening that Johan washed and dressed, he knocked at the door. He was stern but not without empathy. Johan invited him in and he sat down to eat with them.

When they went into the front room for coffee, he asked Johan, "do you blame God?"

"Of course not," answered Johan, "how can I blame God for my mistakes."

"God has forgiven you for your sins because he knows, that in your heart, you are sorry and have asked for forgiveness but, unfortunately, there are always consequences for your actions," said the prophet, "You will have another son and God will bless him,"

After he had left, Johan and Helena held each other. Their love had deepened to something that Johan had never felt before. Could this have been the purpose? Surely God wouldn't take the life of a child to teach his father an important lesson? Could that ever happen?

CHAPTER 20

Trudi had been home for two months now. The people in town had, to a large extent, forgotten about the rape. She went every Sunday to church with Truida and Karl and people greeted her respectfully but Trudi could feel the black mark against her in their minds. Would that ever go away? Trudi, sadly, didn't think so. No man would want her as a wife now. Even if they didn't know about the rape, as soon as they started courting her, all the gossips in the area would be telling her suiter.

Adrian hadn't forgotten. It was still a burning hot coal in his mind. He watched Abri walking around with his friends as if nothing had happened. When Abri did come into contact with Trudi, he looked at her with contempt. Even his friends had the same attitude toward Trudi. Luckily, they didn't see each other very often.

President Thomas François Burgers was hoping to come to some sort of peace agreement with the Pedi, as were the British. Johan, together with Pieter and Kobus, rode out to meet with the British at Ohrigstad to the north. Johan took Adrian with him. The plan was to meet the Pedi paramount chief, king Sekhukhune, and broker a peace agreement between the Pedi, the Boers and the British. They met with Sir Garnet Wolseley in

Ohrigstad and rode together, six in all, to meet the chief.

The chief was all decked out in leopard skins and feathers. He was seated on a stool with five warriors at his back. He didn't get up when Johan's group dismounted. Johan wasn't sure if the king expected them to bow or something but none of them were about to do that. Johan and Wolseley strode forward to a few paces in front of the king.

"King Sekhukhune," said Wolseley, by way of greeting.

The king stood and a warrior took the stool away. Another warrior laid a large grass mat down and Sekhukhune sat, motioning them to sit.

"You have come to see me," said Sekhukhune in English, a statement more than a question.

Johan let Wolseley speak, he could express himself in English better than Johan.

They talked until long after midday. The warriors brought water and sliced fruit to them all. Johan chipped in when he didn't agree but, overall, he thought that the talks went well. The sun was well down toward the horizon when they stood to leave. King Sekhukhune had agreed to stay west of the Steelpoort River.

The delegation rode back into Ohrigstad, to a temporary camp that the British had set up next to the church. Johan guessed there to be about thirty soldiers waiting for Wolseley. They had a fly tent with a table and chairs in the centre of the field and Johan and Adrian, with Pieter and Kobus, followed Wolseley and two other officers to the tent.

Johan was keen to get home before dark but he wanted to talk to Wolseley before leaving.

"I would appreciate your opinion on how the talks went," said Wolseley to Johan when they were seated.

"We have both been in this situation before," answered Johan, "the Pedi didn't keep to their agreement then and I doubt very much if they will keep to it now."

"I agree," said Wolseley resignedly, leaning back on his chair, his pipe in his hand, "I suppose even temporary peace is better than nothing but it is going to come to a decisive campaign, sooner or later. We will have to make ready for that eventuality."

By the time Johan and his men left, the sun had set. Adrian was waiting for an opportune moment to speak to Johan about Abri but Johan was in too much of a hurry to get home. It would have to wait. They rode into Kameelbult after dark.

Adrian was very disgruntled. He had been trying to get Johan to do something about Abri for so long now. He thanked God daily that Trudi wasn't pregnant but there were some people who believed that it was Trudi that seduced Abri when he was at his weakest. It would take some sort of strict, public punishment to convince the town that Abri was the guilty one.

Truida and Karl were sitting in the front room when Adrian walked into the house but Truida came into the kitchen to dish up some stew for Adrian. Adrian first went to wash up.

"How did the meeting go?" asked Truida.

"Very well, I think," answered Adrian, trying to concentrate.

"Have the Bapedi agreed to stop raiding the farms?"

"They have but we know that they don't keep to any agreement. The British don't know them as we do." Adrian's mind was still on Abri.

Karl was watching Adrian intently. He knew something was bothering him. Adrian was actually forming a plan in his mind.

"I can see that you are worried about something," said Karl, "can we help in any way?"

Adrian brightened suddenly, "yes," he said, "I want to hold a party for Trudi's upcoming birthday. She deserves a party."

"Do you think that is wise?" asked Truida, half turning with her hand on the back of a chair.

Karl straightened in his chair, "I think it may be a good idea. The incident has faded in the people's minds by now."

"Where are you thinking of holding the party?" asked Truida, "here?"

"Yes, your front room is as big as a dance hall," answered Adrian, brightening further, "we can invite all off the girls and boys who are around Trudi's age. She knows most of them anyway."

"Don't for a minute think that any boy from this town will want to start courting Trudi, all of a sudden. They won't forget what happened to her," retorted Truida.

"I know that," answered Adrian, "that is not the idea. I only want to cheer her up."

But that wasn't what he was thinking, he was thinking of revenge even though the verses from the apostle Paul's letter to the Romans says 'repay no one evil with evil' was ringing in his ears. This seemed to run in the family, this knowing what they should do but doing something else.

"Settled then?" asked Adrian.

"Yes," answered Truida reluctantly, "I will start making the arrangements."

"I will speak to Trudi," said Adrian, getting up.

He went up the stairs and knocked softly on Trudi's door.

CHAPTER 21

Trudi was alone in the room. She wasn't very excited at first about the party but after a few minutes, started warming to the idea. She started naming girls who she could invite but Adrian told her to make a list. While they were still talking, Rachel came in.

"We are going to need new dresses," said Trudi, excitedly to Rachel.

Looking at Rachel's surprised face she said, "we are going to have a party." Rachel was still trying to get over Adrian's presence.

For a few seconds Adrian forgot what he was doing. He walked through Rachel's smell on his way to the door. He let them get on with it. His plan was now set in motion. Johan had had long enough to put things right. Adrian's brain was in ice-cold mode now. Abri couldn't walk around as if nothing had happened. He was going to pay and pay dearly.

Adrian walked up to Johan's house. The front door was open and Johan and Helena were in the front room. He tapped on the open door to get their attention. He felt sorry for Helena for losing their son, but, hey, Johan had a few more walking around.

"Come in my son," said Johan.

The words grated on Adrian's nerves but he forced himself to smile. "I came to tell you that we are having a party for Trudi's birthday."

Johan turned toward him with a smile, "that is an excellent idea. I don't think I will be able to come but Helena should be there," he said turning expectantly toward Helena.

Helena nodded.

"We are inviting all of Trudi's friends. We are also inviting Abri," continued Adrian.

"Do you think that wise?" asked Johan his smile slipping.

"We must invite all of her friends," said Adrian, purposefully misunderstanding the question.

"I am talking about Abri," said Johan.

"Why, don't you trust him?"

"I mean," answered Johan, dodging the question, "will Trudi even want him there?"

"I think the events have faded in everyone's memories," said Adrian meaningfully but Johan didn't catch the sarcasm. "I think it is time the air was cleared and that Trudi should get closure on the whole incident."

Johan nodded and Helena smiled. So, it was settled. Adrian left Johan's house and walked down the road. He didn't know how he was going to persuade Abri to come to the party.

Abri and Martin were sitting down by the river. From a distance they watched Adrian walking toward Abri's house.

"I think we had better disappear," said Martin, "it looks like Adrian is looking for you."

"Ag, he won't do anything," answered Abri, "he is afraid of his father."

"Your father," said Martin meaningfully, "and you are not?"

"Tsk, anyway, Adrian would have done something by now. His father would also have done something by now," said Abri.

"I guess they must believe the story we told, that Trudi seduced you."

They both laughed.

Adrian saw them sitting down by the river. He turned toward them. He was going to invite them to the party but then decided against it. He thought they may not believe his good intentions. He turned and started up the hill. He decided to ask Truida to invite them through Jaqueline, Abri's mother. When Adrian told Truida she didn't like the idea of inviting Abri but, finally, relented.

So, the party was planned. All of the youngsters in town, who had been at school with Trudi were invited but a number of adults were also invited. Abri's parents were among those invited. Rachel's dad was doing a roaring trade with dresses and material for dresses. Of course, Rachel's parents and Cisca's parents were invited. Adrian doubted very much if Rachel's parents would come to the party. It was going to be held on a Saturday evening, which was the Jewish Sabbath. He hoped that they would allow Rachel to come.

When Jaqueline told Abri, he and Martin were sitting in the front room.

Abri laughed, "you see," he said to Martin, "they have forgotten all about it."

"They want to forget it because they realise that it was Trudi's fault," said Martin, for Jaqueline's sake."

"Are you going to go?" Abri asked Jaqueline.

"Yes, I was also invited."

"I want to wear a blood red shirt," said Abri and Martin laughed, "would you make me one, mother?"

"Yes," said Jaqueline, with a sigh, "but why red?"

Abri and Martin laughed but Abri didn't answer.

Truida reported back to Adrian that Jaqueline and her family had accepted the invitation. The town butcher and baker were also involved in the preparations.

As the date of the party drew near, the town as a whole, became excited. Rachel's parents declined, as Adrian thought they would but they hadn't given a decision on whether Rachel would be allowed to go.

While all this fuss was going on, the town was staggered to hear that Helena was pregnant again. Helena and Johan had kept it secret for as long as possible but, when Helena began to blossom, it became obvious. Even without Helena showing a bump, the servants in town were full of gossip.

Johan told everyone that the prophet had foreseen that it was going to be a boy.

CHAPTER 22

So, the time grew near for the party. Adrian's apprehension was growing. He was formulating the evenings events, step by step, in his mind but of course, only a man with a gift of prophesy could foretell the future and then only what God chose to tell him for the good of someone else. I suppose the Prophet may have known what was going to happen but we don't know why he didn't tell anyone.

It was barely a week to go, when Johan received word that the Pedi were again raiding the farms. Wolseley sent word that he wanted to meet Johan to discuss the situation. The next evening, they met just outside Origstad. So, Johan couldn't go to the party even if he wanted to which, he didn't.

Wolseley was pacing up and down inside the fly tent when Johan arrived with Pieter and Kobus.

"This needs to end once and for all, we have tried three times before but they keep on breaking the treaty."

Johan could have told him that on the day the treaty was signed.

Johan only had fifty men that he could call on at such short notice, "what do you propose?" he asked.

"I have eight hundred Swazis to back us up."

Johan wasn't keen on arming eight hundred Swazis, "do you have rifles for them?"

"Most of them have rifles but they prefer to fight hand-to-hand."

"They will get slaughtered by the Pedi. Most of the Pedi have Mausers now," said Johan.

"I will only send the Swazis in once the Pedi have retreated into the mountains. In the mountains it will be close quarters," argued Wolseley.

Johan had to agree, "where do you want us?"

Kobus was already in the saddle, pulling his horse around to ride to call the rest of the Commando.

"Johan, I would like you in sniper shooting positions, on the rock outcrops surrounding the Pedi camp."

The Boers were renowned for their marksmanship. Johan nodded.

"You should be finalizing your positions at first light." Wolseley was pointing at the map on the table now.

They carried on discussing the attack, "once the Pedi are in the mountains, your men may withdraw. I will hold the Swazis until that stage. They will then push the attack."

Johan had to admit Wolseley was a good military strategist.

Johan's Commando arrived just before midnight. They were already equipped with their ammunition. The British didn't carry Mauser ammunition and so the commando had to carry their own. Their scouts weren't with them. No use putting them at risk if the Boers weren't going to be leading the attack.

Lying in front of the camp fire that night, Johan found sleep difficult to come by. He tried not to think about Helena. Now that she was pregnant again, his heart wasn't here in the moment where it should be. He was glad that Adrian was helping Trudi. He wasn't really sorry that he couldn't be there for the party. He would have liked to see all his children together again. Adrian had asked if he should join the Commando but Johan knew that Adrian wanted to be home with Trudi.

As the morning sky in the east brightened, Johan was already lying on a huge outcrop of rock overlooking the forthcoming battlefield. He cleared the rock surface of dirt next to him and laid his ammunition out, ready to reload. He had wrapped his rifle muzzle in sacking to stop the sun glinting off it and giving away his position. Once he started shooting, the Pedi would look for him and see the puffs of smoke. Smokeless ammunition was still a while in the future.

He licked his thumb and wet the front sight. Each bullet must count. He watched the trees to note the slight breeze blowing across the valley. At this distance the breeze must be taken into account when aiming. He heard the trumpet. Unfortunately, it was the only way of letting the attacking forces know to charge. The Swazis held back but Johan saw the tell-tale puffs of smoke on the outcrops, *koppies*. He methodically aimed and fired, watching his bullets striking home, a brief second delay before the bullet smacked home, due to the distance.

The day went well. The British were outnumbered but, with the Boers sniping, they drove the Pedis back. In the foothills the British allowed the Swazis to forge ahead, pushing into the mountains. Johan and his men rode down into the now deserted valley. Only dead and dying remained.

It was almost midday. Johan had honestly tried to save a few of the wounded Pedi but most, if not nearly all of them were beyond saving. A cry went up from one of the Boers. He beckoned for Johan. When Johan dismounted beside him, he pointed to a body and to a badly wounded Pedi lying next to him.

"This man says that the body is of Sekhukhune's heir, Morwamoche."

Johan was sceptical. It would be unlike the Pedi to leave such an important person behind. He ordered that the body be taken back to Kameelbult. Some of the scouts would be able to make an identification.

By nightfall most of the British were back in camp. Wolseley had left some of his soldiers in the foothills, to watch for any Pedi. He realized that this was dangerous for the Swazis. It would be difficult to distinguish between the Pedi and Swazi.

It was too late for Johan to get back for Trudi's party in Kameelbult, so the commando slept that night in the Origstad camp. Johan was also longing to see his wife again and his mind was on her when he drifted off to sleep.

CHAPTER 23

As the sun went down, Adrian watched the house from up the street. This was going to be a party fit for a king. The people started arriving for the party all dressed in their finery. Adrian didn't want Abri to see him, not yet. He was glad that his father hadn't insisted that he go with the Commando. He was also glad that Johan wasn't here.

The girls had all paraded around the house earlier, showing off their new dresses to each other. Adrian had been standing in the kitchen, pretending to watch the food being prepared. Secretly he was hoping for a glimpse of Rachel.

When she did appear, she was wearing a long purple dress. Her hair, raven black, was tied back with curls hanging down her neck. Adrian was now well and truly in love. He watched her through the open doorway but he tried to stay hidden, his body behind the door, just his head around the doorjamb. When he turned around, one of the kitchen helpers was watching him. She giggled, turned and then went on with cutting vegetables. Adrian felt embarrassed at this and walked outside.

When it became completely dark, Adrian crept back into the house, going from room to room.

Abri hadn't arrived. Rachel looked so ravishing that he nearly neglected to compliment his sister. Trudi did look beautiful. He prayed that Trudi would find someone who would appreciate her regardless of her no longer being a virgin. He knew that there was nothing for God to forgive in her. She was innocent.

Abri and Martin were getting themselves ready at Abri's house. Abri had a full-length mirror attached to his wardrobe in his bedroom. The wardrobe had been a present to him from Johan. Abri stood in front of it now, preening himself. He had his blood-red shirt on. As he looked at himself, he thought that he looked pretty amazing. Hair slicked back and beard trimmed short. He had his father's good looks.

"Ok, let's go," said Martin, lounging on the bed. Martin was wearing a white shirt that he had borrowed from his father but he thought he looked pretty amazing too.

"Ok," said Abri, giving his hair a last flick of the finger.

Martin's boots hit the floor. They picked up their jackets but didn't put them on. It was still hot in the late afternoon. They would put them on as they reached Trudi's house.

"Is your mom and dad coming?" asked Martin.

"They will only come this evening, just before the meal."

They chatted about the meal and about who would be there and what their chances would be with the girls. It was hot in the late afternoon sun as they walked up the hill along the dusty road. Abri was a bit upset that sweat marks were starting to appear under his arms. He had gained weight in the last few months, that wasn't helping.

The place was buzzing when they arrived. Adrian was there greeting the people as they arrived. He greeted Abri and Martin. He seemed to have forgiven Abri. There was a bowl of fruit punch on a table at the entrance. Helping themselves to the punch, Martin and Abri went looking for a cool corner, greeting those they knew along the way. In the corner of the back stoop they found a pile of cushions. From there they could see most of the comings and goings, so they threw themselves down. Still hot, they took their jackets off again. Abri wanted to show off his red shirt, anyway. The smell of the *braai* BBQ in the back garden was drifting through the creepers shading the stoop.

"That smell of the meat on the fire is making me hungry already," said Martin, lifting himself up on one elbow.

Abri was more interested in the girls, "I wonder if we could get one or two of the girls to join us here in the corner of the stoop," he said, "maybe Trudi," he laughed.

"I thought you hated her?" said Martin.

"Hmm, yes I do. Just joking."

They lay back again, looking down the passage at the girls in their finery. Abri could feel himself getting aroused. He would like to get one of the girls back here or, better still, back to his house. His house was empty of people. They were all here. He became more aroused, thinking of what he could do to a girl back there. He started planning his moves.

Adrian circled around and came into the house through the back garden. He didn't want anyone to see him, not yet. He walked past the *braai* fires to the steps up to the stoop. His foot was on the first step when he heard the sound of Abri speaking. He couldn't hear what he was saying but it was definitely Abri's voice.

Abri was in mid-sentence when, suddenly, Adrian stood before him. Martin's mouth dropped open and he stared wide eyed at Adrian bringing his revolver around from behind his back. For a split-second Martin started to relax. The revolver was pointed at Abri. The gun roared in the confined space and then Martin was looking up into the barrel. He had been reaching for his own revolver but had been caught off guard. He wouldn't have thought that Adrian would go for him. Adrian's revolver roared again, deafening in the confined space.

Abri never felt anything. The bullet took him through the frontal lobe giving him a third eye. An extra eye to see him on his way to the judgement seat. The bullets knocked Abri and Martin back against the cushions. Looking real peaceful except for the shock frozen on their faces.

CHAPTER 24

Adrian tucked the revolver into his belt behind his back, under his jacket, as he walked back out, down the steps to the *braai* fires. He didn't look back. If he had, he would have seen Martin moving. The servants cooking at the fires saw Adrian but quickly looked away. They knew what had happened but also knew why it had happened. In fact, they had wondered when it would happen. It had only been a matter of time.

Some of the people had come out the front of the house, the women and girls to get away from the gunfire and the men to see where the gunfire was coming from. Adrian saw Rachel as he whirled his horse around. He lifted his open hand. She lifted hers in return. Then he was riding, the image of the raven-haired beauty burnt into his brain.

He headed north out of town and hoped that someone saw him even though it was already dark. He wanted to give the impression that he was headed north. Johan would soon be after him, of that he was sure. After a few miles he turned west, toward Pretoria. He had friends in Pretoria who would protect him. He also had family there but they had never seen him so there was no chance of them recognizing him in case he was seen in town.

It was already pitch dark. There was no twilight in this part of the world. A flock of guinee-fowl scattered as he thundered down the road. He wanted to get as far as possible away from the scene of the crime. It was not a good idea to be riding in the dark. There were big cats out hunting and he would be riding blind in the thick blackness. The moon would rise later but by then he hoped to have a small fire going. He would have to stop soon.

He rode until he felt that it was no longer safe in the dark. Turning a little way off the road, he unsaddled and wiped his horse down. She was wet with sweat; they had been riding hard. He built a small fire, just big enough to cover with his hat and tried to make himself comfortable.

It was a long ride to Pretoria so there was a lot of time to reflect on what he had just done. He thought, then, that it was justified but a lot of Abri's family would want his blood now, not least of all, Johan. Adrian knew that he had just shot and killed his half-brother. He hoped that Trudi and Rachel would understand. He also wondered if God would ever forgive him. Was murder ever justified. The bible is often misquoted. The commandment is not 'Thou shalt not kill', it is 'Thou shalt not murder' but this was definitely premeditated murder.

After a restless night, he was up again at first light. He knew that Johan wouldn't wait about. He would soon have a commando out after him. Adrian stretched his horse toward Pretoria.

Meanwhile, back in Kameelbult, Rachel was still lying in bed. Her heart was with Adrian. She knew that he loved her, she had seen it in his eyes for some time now. What worried her was how would they get over the fact that she was Jewish and he was a protestant Christian. From birth she had been taught that Jesus was still to come. Would they be able to put aside their differences for the sake of their love for each other?

Rachel knew that Adrian had been the one who had shot Abri and Martin and she could understand why but she wished that he hadn't done it. It had thrown the whole town into a turmoil. Her father was huffing and puffing around the shop this morning and her mother was mumbling to herself. She had no one to speak to about her problems. She knew what their Rabbi would say. She even thought of speaking to the minister of Adrian's church. He seemed a nice man.

Trudi was up early. The body of Abri had been taken away and the house-maid and garden worker had already cleaned the mess on the back stoop. Martin had been taken home, badly wounded. When the shots had been fired, she had run on to the stoop. Peering past the men already there, she had seen the two shot men but couldn't see their faces. The scene that would stay with her for many years was the amount of blood. There was so much blood. All the cushions and bedding had been taken away to be burnt.

Of course, she knew who had done the shooting and who had been shot. Her emotions were running in all directions. She was glad that Abri had finally been brought to justice but death was a very harsh punishment. He would never rape anyone again. And what about Martin? Why did he have to be punished? What was his role in all of this except being Abri's friend? Had he coaxed Abri into it.

Truida seemed to be emotionless, directing the clean-up. Who knew what she was thinking? Actually, she was trying very hard not to be happy. She knew that Abri had not deserved to die. That was very harsh justice but she thought that this was all Johan's fault. He should have brought Abri to justice a long time ago.

Jaqueline had been inconsolable the night before but she was composed the next morning as she walked up to Johan's house. Miriam saw her coming, all dressed in black and she tried to look busy in the kitchen. She knew what this visit was about.

"Where is boss Johan," Jaqueline asked, without a greeting as she walked into the kitchen without even knocking.

"Boss Johan is still on commando," answered Miriam. She wasn't stupid enough to try to be familiar with Abri's mother in this situation. "I don't know when he will be back," she said before Jaqueline could ask.

Jaqueline turned on her heel and walked out without saying another word. As she walked out the gate, Phineas slipped in through the kitchen door, hat in hand.

"Do you think it was Adrian?"

"That's what I was told," answered Miriam.

"And where is Adrian now?"

"Long gone."

Phineas nodded, "good," he said.

CHAPTER 25

Johan was eating breakfast with Pieter and Kobus when a Shangaan tracker rode into camp and walked to where Johan was sitting on a tree stump.

"I come from Kameelbult," he said, "I was told to tell you that your son, Adrian has shot and killed all of your family,"

Johan's blood froze, "what?" he had heard what the Shangaan had said but his brain didn't process it.

The Shangaan stepped back, this looked like a case of the messenger being shot because of the message. He repeated the message but from a safer distance.

"Ja I heard you!" Johan shouted.

The Shangaan beat a hasty retreat.

Johan ran toward the horses, his rifle in hand, "my horse, my horse!" he shouted.

When he swung his horse around, he saw that Pieter and Kobus were also in their saddles. They thundered off at full gallop. Johan was furious but his brain soon started working again. What did he mean when he said 'your whole family'? Did he mean Adrian's whole family? Did he mean Helena? But why would he do that? He slowly came to his senses. He remembered that Adrian had kept nagging him about Abri.

The sweat was streaming off the horses by the time they dusted down the main street of Kameelbult. There were a few people milling around Trudi's house. Martin met them at the door. He had a bandage wrapped around his head.

"Abri?" the question burst from Johan.

"Yes," Martin nodded.

"Who else?"

"And me," said Martin, full of self-pity.

"Tsk! Who else is dead?" exclaimed Johan.

"No-one," said Martin, a bit puzzled at Johan's attitude. He didn't know of the message that Johan had received.

Johan relaxed slightly.

"He killed Abri because of what he did to Trudi," said Martin. He wasn't sure but he thought that is what he should say. He didn't say that he was an inch from being dead too because of the part he had played in the rape of Trudi.

"And Adrian?" asked Johan.

"In the wind. They say he headed north."

Johan turned to Pieter and Kobus, standing behind him, "where would he go north?"

"There is nothing north except wilderness," said Pieter, "unless he knows someone up that way."

"Pieter, Kobus," they knew what he meant and were already running for their horses, Johan and Martin watching them go.

Martin smirked. Adrian would soon face justice for shooting him. He was sure that Adrian had meant to kill him and would have, if he hadn't been in such a hurry. Martin knew that it was only him half turning to reach for his gun that had saved him.

Truida walked into the room but Johan turned abruptly and walked out. The sweat was still dripping off his horse as he climbed into the saddle again. He took it slow now, walking his horse to cool her off, up to his house. Phineas took the horse without a word and led her to the barn. Helena met him on the stoop and fell into his arms with a sob.

Johan's mind was in a whirl. He wasn't sure how he felt. Glad that no-one else in his family had been shot but his heart ached, not just for his son Abri but also for his son Adrian.

CHAPTER 26

It was the beginning of autumn. It could get cold in Pretoria. The Barron family lived on the east side of town, just up the road from the Lion Bridge. Adrian came in from the east, walking his horse down Church Street. Two young boys were playing near to the road and Adrian stopped to ask them where the Barrons lived. The boys were wearing shorts and bare-foot, even though it was autumn. He knew approximately where the house was but wasn't sure. The boys pointed to a large house nearby. Adrian swung up and noticed the boys following him. There was a hitching rail near the front door. One of the boys, about ten years old, took the reins from him.

A woman was watching from the doorway. Adrian climbed the few steps to the stoop and doffed his hat as he approached the woman.

"Good evening aunty," he greeted her.

He noticed the rifle hanging half hidden behind her dress. Out the corner of his eyes he saw the boys spread out, one on each side, slightly behind him. Adrian kept his hands clear of his clothing, not wanting to give the wrong impression.

"Good evening," she answered. Friendly enough but cautious.

"Adrian Venter, aunty. I am looking for my cousins, the Barrons."

"Well you had better not call me aunty again," she snorted. "I am Sharon Jamima Barron."

She turned and walked into the house, "come in," she said over her shoulder.

Adrian felt the atmosphere relax as the boys climbed the steps behind him.

"*Dag Oom,*" the boys said in unison and followed him into the house.

When the woman reached the kitchen she turned, "I am your cousin, Sharon. This is Jerry and Joel. My husband, Josh, is trying to help sort out a conflict brewing between the Boers and the British. Some talk of the British wanting to annex the Transvaal."

She replaced the rifle on a rack above the back door and turned to the stove, "sit," she said over her shoulder. It was a big stove and gave off quite a lot of heat, welcomed in this weather.

She put a cup of coffee down in front of Adrian. The aroma coming off the cup was something from heaven. Adrian put his cold hands around the hot cup. The warmth coming from the stove and the warmth of the people was putting a new look on this day.

"I thought we were friends with the British now. I was with my father just a few days back, speaking with the British?" Adrian was genuinely shocked, "although I don't suppose the army knows what the politicians are doing."

"Yes, well, things have changed with the discovery of diamonds in the west. Josh is an advocate, well thought of by both parties but he doesn't hold out much hope for a peaceful outcome."

Sharon didn't ask Adrian why he was there. Adrian was thankful for that. If Josh was a well thought of advocate, he might feel it his duty to bring Adrian before the law.

Adrian stayed with Josh and Sharon for the winter. The murder still weighed heavily on his mind. There was no doubt that he had meant to kill Abri but now that it was done, he started doubting whether it was the right thing to have done. Before the shooting, anger had burned deep inside of him. Was there such a thing as a 'righteous kill'? One evening, when Josh had read the family bible after supper, Adrian asked his opinion.

"Well, there is nothing to support it in the teaching of Jesus." That was an advocate's opinion. They did find, in the letter of Paul to the Romans, 'do not repay evil with evil.' But Adrian already knew that.

Adrian struggled to sleep that night. There were two things keeping him awake now, the shooting (he didn't want to call it murder) and his longing for Rachel. He should have told her how he felt before he left Kameelbult.

Unbeknown to him though he was spotted in Pretoria by Pieter who had come to Pretoria on instructions of Johan to find out what was happening with the British. So far, in Kameelbult, they had only heard rumours of war, no drums yet.

Pieter didn't make this finding known but he did find out that the famous advocate, Josh Barron, was cousin to Adrian. That would make Johan, uncle by marriage to Josh. But Pieter was very fond of Adrian, Adrian and Trudi, as a matter of fact. He had watched them growing up and he knew them to be loving, respectful and of good manners. He had been upset with the whole episode of the rape of Trudi and he himself had been waiting for Johan to bring justice to the matter. He didn't know that Abri was also Johan's son. When Adrian had shot Abri, Pieter wasn't surprised. He didn't condone it but he did understand it.

Pieter stayed in Pretoria for the whole month of August but by the end of that time, it was obvious that the British were determined to annex the Transvaal to obtain the rights to the diamond find.

Pieter rode back to Kameelbult with this bad news of the hostile British weighing him down. Also, on his mind, was the matter of Adrian. How was he going to tell Johan that Adrian was in Pretoria? September was supposed to be a happy month. Spring was in the air. All around a new age was beginning. Buds on the trees which would soon blossom, turning the streets of Pretoria mauve with colour of the Jacaranda flowers.

As Pieter rode up the street to Johan's house, he formulated a plan. Not really unique, this plan had been used on Johan once before but Pieter didn't know that. Johan had never told anyone how the prophet had tricked him into convicting himself.

Phineas ran out to take Pieter's horse and when he walked into the kitchen, he could smell fresh coffee brewing. Johan hurried to meet him and Helena, heavy with child, kissed him on the cheek before leaving the men to men's business. Pieter and Johan sat opposite each other and took a sip of hot coffee before getting down to business.

CHAPTER 27

Johan and Pieter spoke about the hostilities with the English, British actually but to the Boers, anyone who spoke English was an *Engelsman*. Pieter never mentioned the fact that he had seen Adrian. The sun was setting by the time Pieter shook Johan's hand on the stoop and walked to where Phineas was holding his horse. He rode out with a plan already finalized in his mind.

He rode to Katelina's house. Now he knew Katelina from childhood, *his* childhood. Katelina, or Kat, as everyone in Kameelbult knew her. She was older than Pieter by about ten years but she was someone who everyone in town knew because she was said to be a Lesbian and so scorned by most people for most of her life. There had even been talk of her being stoned but Johan and others had threatened to hunt anyone down who harmed her.

Now that she was much older, she had been finally accepted by most of the community. She was still a loner and she hunted in the mountains alone. Pieter had secretly befriended her when he was still a teenager and knew her to have a loving heart.

It was dark when Pieter rode up to her door. There was a lamp burning in the front room and the smell of cooking drifted out to him. She opened the door to him and ushered him in. Another old lady was sitting in the front room and stood to leave when he walked in. He was surprised to see that it was the old Jewess who he always assumed was Rachel's grandmother. He waited politely for her to leave and Kat took him to the kitchen.

"There is something that I need you to do for me but not just for me."

Kat listened to what he had to say, nodding as he spoke.

"Of course," she said finally.

When Pieter stood to leave, she put her hand on his arm, "would you keep an old lady company and share a meal with me?" she asked.

Well, Pieter was starving and the aroma coming from the pots on the stove was already making his mouth water.

"What you have asked me to do, I will do with pleasure," she said slowly. She always spoke slowly, making sure that her audience understood he perfectly. This was the reason that Pieter had chosen her for the task.

"The woman who just left is Rachel's grandmother," she confirmed. "We have another problem to find a solution to."

Pieter's interest was aroused.

"It seems that Rachel is in love with Adrian and it seems that her feelings may be reciprocated. Not as big a problem as I had when younger but still a problem. We have a Jewish girl in love with a gentile boy."

"Does any-one else know about this?" he asked.

"Not that I know of," she said. "Ruth, her grandmother, says that Rachel confided in her and very tearfully too."

"Well, an almost impossible situation," Pieter's heart was sinking. His heart felt heavy for the boy. "One of them is going to have to make a life-wrenching change. Whoever changes, is going to bring the wrath of their family down on them."

"Maybe not," said Kat, "Ruth seems to think that, with some very careful talking, Rachel's father may accept it."

"Less painful for Adrian," said Pieter, tongue in cheek, "but what about Rachel's beliefs."

"Jesus being a Jew is a good start," said Kat, "the *dominee* would need to get involved. Rachel's father is the first hurdle though."

Pieter nodded, "but let's get Adrian home first."

They ate in silence. It was late when Pieter rode up the street toward his house. So many problems to sort out. Without his faith, he would have despaired.

CHAPTER 28

Kat knew what she had to do. She wasn't worried about-facing Johan. He had always supported her in spirit. What she was worried about was tricking him. She didn't know that he had been tricked before. She first sent a message to him, asking when he would be available to talk about a problem.

The next evening, she walked into Johan's front room. She was met by Johan and Helena. Kat was dressed in her men's trousers and white lace top with a heavy black cape thrown over her shoulders. Her grey hair was pulled back from her face. No matter what she did, she still looked like a beautiful woman, thought Johan. He took her cape and kissed her on the cheek.

They sat drinking a liqueur, distilled here in Kameelbult, while they chatted about their lives. Helena had been part of that childhood and joined in the conversation. Miriam called them into the dining room as the aroma of good cooking drifted through the house. Miriam knew Kat. She had been to Kat for advice many times and had received wise help every time.

After supper they moved into the front room again for coffee. Helena then left them. She knew that Kat would only open up to Johan when they were alone. Finally, Johan asked Kat how he could help.

"Someone came to see me," she said, "her sons got into a fight over a woman."

Johan smiled. Why else would two men fight.

"The one struck the other, once too often," she continued, "the punch killed him."

Johan leaned forward. This was serious. "Was this lately?"

Kat nodded. "He went on the run; some say up north. Some say out west. His mother wants to bring him home but her husband says he will kill him if he sees him again. If that happens, they will have no children and she is too old to bear children. Her husband has more than one wife, one who is young and could give birth at any time"

"How would I be able to help?" asked Johan.

"This woman's husband respects you and will do anything you ask," Kat said.

Johan felt his ego rise. That a man would do anything he asked. He couldn't help but feel puffed up.

"If you could speak to this man please, she will be very grateful."

"Of course, I will," said Johan. "Do I know this man? Show him to me and I will make sure that nothing happens to the boy. Who is this man?"

"It is you Johan."

Johan nearly fell out of his chair. He realised now that he had been tricked once again.

"Why do you refuse to let your son come home?" Kat was pressing him now.

Johan hung his head for a few moments.

"Kat you misunderstand me," he said, looking up. "There is nothing more I would rather do, but," he held his hand up, palm facing toward her, "the law would require that he be tried for murder. There are witnesses."

"Tsk," Kat blew between her teeth, "you are the law here Johan. The people will listen to you."

Johan suddenly realised by whom he had been tricked. "Did Pieter put you up to this?"

"Whether he did or not is beside the point," said Kat, "what I am saying is true and very important, Maybe the most important thing in your life right now."

Johan sat back. So, it was Pieter. But what she said was true. He hung his head again. When he looked up again, his eyes were slightly bloodshot.

"If I do this, I will have to find a very good excuse to put to the community."

"Blame it on the coming war," said Kat. "You need every able-bodied man that you can get right now. You can say that you will sort out his punishment later, as you put off Abri's punishment"

Johan thought for a few minutes, "but I don't know where he is."

"Tsk," Kat blew through her teeth again, "you know that Pieter knows."

Yes, he did know that Pieter knew. He looked hard at Kat. He really admired this woman. Not in a way that he usually admired women, almost like a sister.

"Would you tell Pieter to come and see me, please?" he asked her.

When she was leaving, he kissed her on the cheek again.

"You are not angry with me?" she asked, glancing sideways at him.

"Never," he said, "and you are always welcome in this house."

It was the next morning that Pieter came to see him.

CHAPTER 29

The three girls were crying in Trudi's bedroom again, this time crying for Rachel. Trudi and Ciska were trying to comfort Rachel but were crying as much as she was. The way they saw things, she was in an impossible situation. Her parents would never allow Rachel to marry Adrian. It was bad enough that she spent so much time with her gentile friends, although they did realise that there weren't many options available. There was only one other Jewish family in Kameelbult and their children were not even teenagers yet. Rachel's mother, Ruth, was a bit softer on the idea than her father but never-the-less she wouldn't take to the idea. Of course, they weren't aware yet of the events taking place.

They didn't even know where Adrian was or even if he would ever come back to Kameelbult. He may get sent to trial for murder in Pretoria, if Johan got hold of him. The girls tried to find out if any of their friends knew where he was hiding out but Adrian had always been a bit of a loner. Rachel was willing to run away and hide out with him, if she only knew where he was.

Eventually it was Fredrik Lotz who came to her one evening. She was sitting on the stoop when Fred came in off the street. He had seen her from the street and they had waved to each other. They had been to school together.

"Come sit." said Rachel. It wasn't like Fred to visit so Rachel knew that he must have something that he wanted to say. "Would you like coffee?" she asked.

He shook his head, "I heard you were looking for Adrian?" he asked softly. He knew that this was a forbidden subject, in this house anyway.

Rachel didn't say anything.

"I saw him in Pretoria," said Fred, "but how long he will stay there, I don't know. There are hostilities brewing with the English and he may join a Commando."

"I want to go to him," said Rachel, pleading in her voice. They were talking very softly.

"What about your father?"

"I will leave without his knowledge."

"I am going to Pretoria on the Zederburg coach at daybreak," said Fred. "If you come with me, I will show you where he is staying."

A Zederburg coach trip was an adventure in itself in those days. It was a two-day journey from Lydenburg. Stopover for the night at a cabin but the cabin usually had warm food and a toilet, not too far from the back door of the cabin. It was advisable to take a shotgun when you went at night. Then there were the elephants that thought they owned the road. Sometimes a deviation had to be made at speed.

Rachel told her mother she was going but said she was going to visit her aunt in Pretoria. She made her mother promise not to say anything to her father until he arrived home that evening. By then she would be out of his reach. She didn't want her mother to worry too much, although she would anyway. She went in to Lydenburg with her father but said she was spending the day with a friend, all justifiable lying.

She left on the coach from Lydenburg early the next morning. The coach made good time. No elephants on the road. Fred rode up top to give more room for the ladies inside. Uncle Dries was driving the coach, not her real uncle but everyone called him uncle. It was dark by the time they reached the half-way cabin. When they were climbing out of the coach, they could already smell the hot stew. The ladies had to take turns to the toilet, the men didn't have that problem. The food tasted good and the coffee, magic. After two cups of coffee, Rachel needed to go to the out-house again.

The shot-gun hung over the back door. Rachel had hunted guinee-fowl and ducks many times with her father so the gun felt comfortable under her arm as she cautiously walked the path to the little wooden shed, storm lantern in one hand. She lay the shot-gun on the bench beside her. The smell in the shed wasn't too pleasant but tolerable. She was hardly seated when the door burst open and a man made a grab for her.

CHAPTER 30

The first recorded use of the word *shotgun* was in Kentucky in 1776, however fire-arms that functioned as what we now call shotguns, predate that by centuries, having been used before the cast bullet was invented.

Anyway, back to the toilet. The gun came into her hands from her side as if it was born there but the man was quick. He had his arms around her, crushing her to him with the shotgun between them as he lifted her off the seat. Rachel's finger was already on the trigger. She leaned her head back, closed her eyes and squeezed.

The blast was deafening in the confined space and half the roof disappeared. So did the man's scull. Rachel was showered with blood. The brains went the way of the roof. The man fell back, out of the door, down the step. Rachel tidied herself, she hadn't even had time for a decent wee. Rachel felt badly shaken.

The back door of the cabin erupted with men. The men almost carried her back into the brightly lit cabin, enquiring all the way as to her good health. There was a bustle and humdrum as to what had happened and who the man was or had been. Seems nobody knew him except for his name on the passenger list, not on Rachel's coach but the one going in the opposite direction, from Pretoria to Komatipoort. The man with half a head was carried off.

Fred buzzed around trying to make sure that Rachel was not harmed. A woman from Rachel's coach took her outside, carrying Rachel's bag with her and helped her to clean off at the water trough outside. She had to change her dress and stick her head under the water so that the woman could wash the blood out of her hair. The water was cold but it helped to shock her back to reality.

The woman's name was Rabecca, known as Becky to her friends. Wonders of wonders, she was Jewish. She and Rachel clicked immediately. Rachel wondered later, if God hadn't had something to do with this chance meeting. Maybe not the attack though. It wasn't long before Rachel poured out her story.

"Would you consider staying with my husband and I in Pretoria," asked Becky, after listening carefully to the story.

"My aunt is expecting me."

"We can let her know. Do you think she will mind?" asked Becky.

So it was settled.

The next morning Fred sat on top now as the coach thundered toward Pretoria. It was hot and dusty in the coach and Rachel wished that she could ride on top too but, of course, she was a woman. Becky sat opposite her. It was impossible to hold a conversation in the coach but still possible to shout to each other. There was a man dressed in a brown pin-striped suit with his wife sitting opposite him, middle aged. Rachel hadn't heard them say a word to each other. She knew they were man and wife because of the coach-man calling them all together to board.

They stopped briefly to water the horses and then thundered on. The rivers all had low bridges but there hadn't been any heavy rains lately. The road was rocky in some places but otherwise they made good time and careered into the square in front of Pretoria station late afternoon. A spider carriage with driver was waiting for Becky.

Becky spoke to the driver in South Sotho and he collected their bags. The ride took them out of Pretoria central, north in the direction of the Poort but stopped at a large house just before the road rose to go over the pass. Rachel stood looking at the house before Becky linked her arm and guided her toward the front door. From the size of the house and the furnishings, it was obvious that these people were very rich.

Becky introduced Rachel to her husband, Paul, before showing her to her room. There was a basin and a tall jug of water in her room so Rachel was able to freshen up before wandering out to look for Becky. Supper was a very formal affair.

They had been keen to get home before the start of the Jewish Sabbath. The next morning, they rode up the hill toward the Synagogue passing the Christian church in Andries street. The church was empty, it being Saturday, but the doors were standing open. Rachel peered in the doors at the top of the steps, as they rode past. She knew in her heart that Adrian wouldn't be there but she couldn't help looking. The Synagogue was next to a park and over the road from the prison that would, not many years later, hold Winston Churchill, the news-paper correspondent.

CHAPTER 31

Approximately one thousand, nine hundred years previously, a Roman centurion walked up the hill outside the city wall to where his men were still on duty. Three men had been crucified that day. Two robbers and another man, the centurion wasn't sure what crime the third man had been convicted of. Two women and a man stood nearby and shrank back as he walked toward them. The place stank of garbage and rotting flesh. This was the city dump.

"Are they dead yet?" he called to his men.

One of the men turned and walked toward him. "no Centurion."

"Well, break their legs," he ordered.

He knew that the men being crucified would have tried to hold their bodies erect in order to breath. By breaking their legs, the men on the crosses would slump forward, so putting weight on the lungs and suffocating them. The men jerked up as the soldier broke their legs with a pole, as if screaming silently and then slumping forward.

When they came to the third one, the soldier with the pole peered up. "this one is already dead," he said.

The centurion took a spear from one of the soldiers standing nearby. He shoved the spear up under the man's ribcage until the spearhead almost disappeared into his body. When he pulled it out, a small amount of blood and water flowed out. Enough to spill onto the centurion's arm. The women, standing nearby, now sobbed loudly. The man with the women tried to console them. The centurion glanced up at the board above the man's head, at the top of the cross. It read, in Latin, THE KING OF THE JEWS. The Jewish leaders had wanted it to read HE SAYS HE IS THE KING OF THE JEWS but the Roman governor had ordered that it not be changed.

Normally, the bodies would have been taken down and thrown on the heap but someone had requested that the third man be handed over to him for burial and the governor had consented. Apparently, this man who had made the request was of some importance. The centurion couldn't wait to get off the hill, aptly called 'The Hill of Skulls' or 'Golgotha'. He knew that it would take weeks before the stench would finally disappear completely from his tunic.

"There was an earth-quake earlier, just when this third man died, and the sky turned black," said one of the soldiers, "he shouted something in Aramaic."

"I felt the earthquake, just a normal occurrence. You have been working with the dead too long," but as he walked away, the centurion had a strange feeling that he had witnessed an event that was beyond normal.

It was three woman who had followed Jesus all the way from Galilee to Jerusalem the previous week, the two Marys and Salome. The fearless devotion of these women stands out. They remained with Christ when the male disciples ran for their lives.

The dead men were taken down and the third man was taken away to be sealed in a tomb prepared for him. A huge rock was rolled in front of the entrance by two soldiers.

The Jews had wanted this done before the start of the Passover. In the same way Rachel and Becky wanted to be home before the start of the Sabbath. Rachel had a strange feeling as they rode on up the hill toward the synagogue.

That afternoon, Fred approached the front door of the Barron's house. He wasn't sure what he was going to say to Adrian. It was Sharon who answered the knock. The two boys came charging through.

"Hey, where are your manners!" she called after them.

Then she turned toward Fred, "good afternoon," she said, "how can I help."

"I am looking for Adrian Schultz," he said.

"I am afraid he left this morning at daybreak. A man from the Lydenburg Commando called on him and they left together."

He turned away, after thanking the woman. What was he going to tell Rachel? She had come all the way to Pretoria for nothing and he felt partly responsible. It was now well into the afternoon. Adrian would be halfway to Kameelbult by nightfall. If he left immediately, Fred would reach them before they broke halfway camp in the morning. But was it worth it? He decided to just confront Rachel with the bad news and, maybe, offer to escort her back home.

Sharon stared after the man. He had seemed disturbed by the news of Adrian's departure She shrugged, turned and walked back into the house, shouting after the boys, Joel and Jerry. She wiped her hands on her apron, Josh would be home soon and she still needed to cook his supper.

CHAPTER 32

But Adrian hadn't left for home. After leaving the house with Pieter, he had taken him into town, He showed him where a Commando was gathering on the town square.

"I have formed my own commando," Adrian said, "we are leaving immediately to confront the English at *Amajuba*. I can't go home now. We have a new enemy."

Pieter secretly agreed with him but his orders, as he saw it, was to persuade Adrian to return home. Adrian wasn't about to go home. As far as he knew, his father still wanted to arrest him in spite of what Pieter told him.

During the time Adrian had been in Pretoria, he had gathered men around him. They were now ready to ride west to *Amajuba*, the Hill of Doves. The British forces were led by a Colley General George Pomeroy-Colley (no relation to the author please). The biggest mistake Colley made was not dragging artillery up the hill. Adrian and his men arrived at *Amajuba* shortly before daybreak after riding through the night.

"We are organizing the commandoes into a storming party," a man said to him as he swung off his horse, "Nicolaas Smit is organizing the party. Your commando will be commanded by Field Cornet Roos."

"How many men do we have altogether?" asked Adrian.

"About four hundred, maybe more."

"And the British?

"About the same. The ladies from hell are also there," the man said with a smirk, referring to the Gordon Highlanders, wearing kilts. "Commandant Malan and Commandant Ferreira are leading the other two groups."

Adrian's men gathered around Smit as he gave last minute instructions, "be careful of cannon fire," he said, "fire at will but make every shot count."

The sun was about to break over the hills as they slowly made their way up the slope, taking advantage of every bit of cover. They kept up a constant fire, picking off the enemy as they went. The Highlanders were shouting and firing but they, themselves, never dug in nor used the cover.

Roos shouted continuously to his men in Afrikaans, organising a blanket of fire while groups crossed open ground. Around midday Ferreira's men finally charged the knoll and captured it. That wasn't the end. The Highlanders were still shooting bravely but the Boers were better shots and slowly advanced.

Adrian hugged the rocks. Bullets were pinging of the rocks but the shooting was too high. Even so, some were managing to find their mark and some of Adrian's men went down. A sharp piece of rock whacked Adrian on the head and blood trickled down his face. The cut stung with sweat. Those Jocks were courageous but were no match to the Boers when it came to shooting. It was hard, sweaty work. Dust got into every nook and cranny. Adrian felt sand inside his boots but there was nothing that he could do about it.

This was far different from fighting the Pedi and Adrian felt that any second could be his last. He watched one of his men break cover and run toward the next rock but he didn't make it. His head popped like a watermelon. Another one followed him. A small puncture wound in front but a cauliflower of blood out the back.

When nightfall came, the British took advantage of the dark and began to slip away. By this time, the Boers had almost encircled the mountain with reinforcements arriving right through the day.

Colley (not related to the author remember) was shot and killed. Adrian heard later that nearly three hundred British had been killed or wounded in that battle. Only thirty Boers died in the battle for *Amajuba.* But even those few were too many. Thirty women would be mourning by tomorrow night. That was the inevitability of war, people died.

As he wandered around the *braai* fires that night, listening to the festivities, he noticed how many teenage boys, some not older than thirteen, were celebrating with them. He had seen some of these boys on the slopes, picking off the British soldiers.

Almost a hundred men gathered around Adrian the next morning. He was now a seasoned warrior, worthy of respect and worthy as a leader.

During this time that Adrian had been at Majuba, Johan and his commando had been with other Boer commandoes laying siege to the town of Lydenburg, A garrison of British troops under Lieutenant Long were holed up there after they had been driven there by about five hundred Boers who now surrounded the place.

After the battle of Majuba, Johan and other Boer commanders rode into Lydenberg under a white flag and told Long that Major-General George Pomeroy-Colley (not related to the author) had been killed. They requested that he surrender but it took Long another week to admit defeat. The siege lasted for eighty-four days and tied up hundreds of Boers who could have been fighting elsewhere. This was a lesson that cost the Boers dearly later-on.

CHAPTER 33

When Pieter walked into the front yard at Johan's house, it looked like organised chaos. He grabbed Phineas, who was almost running, backwards and forwards, "what is going on?"

"Boss Johan is leaving town.!"

"Why?"

Phineas shrugged and walked away. Pieter went up the front steps, across the stoop and into the house. Johan was bustling around.

"What's going on?" Pieter asked loudly.

"Adrian has gathered some men and is coming back to Lydenburg," Johan said without stopping, "he surely means to kill me. Adrian hates me for not taking action against Abri over the rape scandal. Now he is riding back here at the head of more than a hundred men. I don't want to clash with him. He is my son and I love him."

Pieter grabbed Johan's sleeve as he was walking past, "I spoke to Adrian," said Pieter, "he told me that he loves you. He wouldn't do anything against you. Yes, he is angry and unhappy about the way you handled the whole affair but he won't do anything rash, I am sure of it."

But Johan was having none of it. Helena and Miriam were rushing backward and forward, carrying clothes and linen. By sundown the wagons were loaded.

"When do you expect Adrian?" Pieter asked. He was still there watching the goings on.

"I don't know," said Johan, "but we are leaving at sunrise."

"But where will you go?" Pieter asked.

This is not the Johan that I grew up with and followed into battle, thought Pieter. He looked at him, at his thinning hair and white flecks in his beard. He turned away, saddened by what he was witnessing. He arrived home and hugged his wife long and hard.

She could sense that something was wrong, "what is it Pieter?"

"We have lost a great leader," he said, "I hope that Adrian is man enough to fill his boots." He felt a sob coming on. I must be getting old and soft myself, he thought.

Before Johan went to bed, he called Miriam and Phineas to the kitchen.

"Miriam, Phineas," he said, "I want you to stay here when we leave."

They started to protest but he held up his hand to stop them, "I want you both to do something for me. Serve Adrian well, but, keep your ears open. If you hear anything about me. Send me a message. I am taking a body-guard of Swazi warriors with me. The Swazi captain from the commando will know where I am. No one else will know."

The next morning at day-break, the wagon pulled out of the yard. The Swazis joined him as they rumbled through town. They were almost out of Kameelbult town when a man stepped out in front of the wagon.

"You are a murderer and now you run!" the man screamed, lifting a rifle to his shoulder.

The Swazi leader surged forward, bring his rifle up.

"No!" shouted Johan at the Swazi. Much softer he said, "he won't shoot."

It was Martin, "it was because of your sloppiness that Abri was murdered!" he shouted at Johan.

Johan climbed off the wagon and walked to Martin. Martin was sobbing now.

As Johan reached Martin, he dropped the muzzle of the rifle that had been pointing at Johan, "he was my friend," Martin sobbed.

Johan couldn't help himself, he put his arms around Martin and hugged him, "and he was my son," he sobbed softly in Martin's ear.

Johan didn't see the knife in Martin's hand. He only felt the cold steel. But Martin had stabbed too low. The blade went into Johan's hip cutting into the muscle and sinew, finally hitting the hip joint. Johan pushed him away, the shock at what had happened, shielded him from pain but he heard the shot from the Swazi that took Martin between the eyes.

Johan and Martin fell to the ground together. In less than a minute, they were both picked up. The Swazis bundled Johan into the wagon. They threw Martin into the back as the driver cracked his whip and they rumbled on. Helena was already busy beside Johan with torn cloths, red with blood.

They crossed into Mozambique late afternoon and turned north. Johan had friends who would keep him protected and secret but he needed immediate medical attention. His wound was deep, not life threatening but he would never walk without a limp. Their destination was the farm of a man who had known Johan from before the English had started their slow infiltration. Willem Bester, now a cattle farmer of some renown in Mozambique, Willem enjoyed a peaceful life with no trouble from the local Shangaans. Martin's body was still in the back of the wagon.

Johan promised himself and God that he would give Martin a Christian burial. He never realized that his move to Mozambique would be the forerunner of many Boers, forced out of their home country by the English.

CHAPTER 34

Adrian was oblivious to all the excitement in his name. He came back to Kameelbult wanting to speak to the Prophet and then to the *dominee*. There were so many things on his mind. Not least of all was Rachel. He didn't want to speak to Johan right away so he went straight to the *dominee*. If he had known of the commotion, he would have first tried to get a message to Johan. He loved Johan and would never have thought of going against him.

There was no one at the church office. He was about to mount when he saw someone walking amongst the tomb-stones. Adrian walked into the graveyard and found the *dominee* standing in front of a grave. He glanced at the stone and saw that the surname was the same as the *dominee*. It was a girl who had died at the age of ten.

The *dominee* didn't turn toward Adrian, "we must all die," he said., still with his back toward Adrian.

"Yes Dominee," said Adrian, doffing his hat.

"But we don't know why some must die so young." The *dominee* turned now, took Adrian's elbow and started walking toward the church.

Adrian allowed himself to be guided up the slight slope, "I need to talk to you *Dominee*."

"Yes, of course."

The church was cool. Hardwood pews made here in Kameelbult and flat cushions also made here.

They sat at the back and the *dominee* turned to Adrian, "what is it *Neef* (nephew)."

"You know what has happened in town?"

"I know what has happened. There are a number of things that have happened but what do you need?"

"Forgiveness, I suppose."

"I can't forgive you," said the *dominee*, "only God can."

"Can't you speak to God for me? You must have direct access to Him? Maybe I should speak to the Prophet"

"Adrian, Jesus died so that we all can have direct access to God," said the *dominee*. "That is the whole reason that he came and died. So that anyone who believes in Him can have a direct relationship with God and have eternal life."

"What must I do then *Dominee,*" Adrian was close to tears now.

"If you are truly sorry for what you have done, tell Him and He will forgive you."

"Very well."

"Well do it then!"

"I am!" Adrian was leaning with his forehead against the pew in front of him with his eyes closed.

The *dominee* waited.

Adrian sat back, "what now?" he asked, "how do I know that he has forgiven me?"

"Because He promised that if you truly meant it, you will be forgiven."

Adrian had been all wound up, now he relaxed. "I do have another problem."

The *dominee* almost laughed out loud, "now what is it?"

"I am in love with a Jewish girl," he said.

"That is not a sin."

"But she is Jewish and I am not."

"Jesus was also a Jew," said the *dominee.*

"Dominee you are not making this easy for me."

The *dominee* smiled with compassion, "it is not an easy problem to solve. The problem is not with God or on your side and so not for God or you to solve. Her family are definitely going to be against the marriage, but I have no doubt, that if you love each other, you will find a way."

Adrian wasn't sure that it was going to be that simple. Adrian felt as if he was flying. He couldn't wait to see Rachel. His horse thundered up the street. He had to get cleaned up first. He smelt like a pig. Phineas took his horse as he rode into the yard in a cloud of dust. He pulled off his shirt and almost dived into the trough.

Since riding with the commando, it had become a habit of his to leave clean clothes at his father's house.

Miriam ran down to the trough, "Rather let me pour a hot bath for you. That trough is not going to make you clean."

He drew his head out of the water, looked at her and nodded. As he walked up to the house, he couldn't help wondering where Johan was. He had expected to be accosted by Johan by now.

It wasn't long before he was in clean clothes, hair slicked down and beard trimmed. He strode out into the yard where Phineas was holding one of the spare horses from the stable. Adrian missed a beat in his stride, because of Phineas' actions but also looking around for Johan.

"Your horse is tired," said Phineas, "I have rubbed him down and put him in the stable."

Adrian nodded, "Thank you," he said, as he swung into the saddle. "Where is Johan?" he asked as he was about to ride off. Phineas just shook his head.

Adrian took this to mean that Johan was away somewhere. He didn't notice that he had already taken over Johan's position as leader.

He wasn't in a hurry anymore as he walked the horse to Rachel's house. He was about to go into the house when Fredrick came walking past. He actually did walk past, did a double take and came back.

"I thought it was you," he said, knowing why Adrian was there, "Rachel isn't here."

"What do you mean?" asked Adrian, a bit rattled, "where is she?"

So, Fred had to tell him the whole story, slowly, from the start, from the leaving without her father's knowledge. Adrian groaned. He looked around. It was already too late to leave for Pretoria, although he was tempted and burning to jump into the saddle. The sun had already headed for its bed.

He headed back to Johan's house and moped around until Miriam called him to supper in the kitchen. He had only just finished eating when Pieter walked in. Before he could say a word, Adrian invited him to sit for coffee. And so, Pieter gave him the whole story that Johan had left so as not to have to clash with Adrian.

Adrian pushed his chair back and put his head in his hands. Although Pieter knew where Johan had gone, he didn't know about the stabbing.

"Please get word to him. He is my father and I would never clash with him even if we have had our differences. I am sure we can work this out."

Pieter nodded, "I will ride with you in the morning. I know where Rachel is living but the family may be a problem, they don't take kindly to Gentiles meddling. We may have to lure her away so that you can speak to her in private."

CHAPTER 35

A certain Mr Harrison had sold his legitimate, registered gold claim for £10 before disappearing. The claim, south of Johannesburg started the gold rush. Cecil John Rhodes registered "The Gold Fields of South Africa" in London, with his brother Thomas as the first chairman, sparking the controversy which, arguably led to the second war with the South African Republic, called the *Zuid Afrikaanse Republiek* and the *Oranje Vrystaadt*.

By the time Adrian and Pieter reached Pretoria, the clouds of war were gathering. Adrian met with the men who had served with him in the first war against the English. Some were missing, age catching up with them. Pieter would have loved to have ridden with them but he was afraid that he would slow them down. He was older than the oldest. Little did he know that it wouldn't be long before old men and boys would be fighting alongside in the war that dragged on for three years.

Before Adrian rode off, he wanted to see Rachel. He didn't know what her feelings were for him. He had seen her smile at him with a smile that had made is heart want to burst but a long time had passed since they had spoken. He was also not sure what she would think about marrying a

Gentile one day. He hoped to tell her that he would come back for her one day. Of course, he didn't know what the outcome of the war would be or how long it would last. The Boers had beaten the English once before so there was nothing to suggest that they wouldn't do it again.

Pieter rode with him to the front of the house in Pretoria where Rachel was staying but that was as far as he was prepared to go. Adrian had never been so scared in his life. Facing this house was worse that facing the screaming soldiers from hell. He climbed down at the entrance to the property and slowly walked his horse up the road to the front of the house. A woman answered the knock on the open door.

"Rachel please aunty," Adrian asked respectfully in Dutch.

"Sorry," she answered in English, "she left this morning for Kameelbult." She watched him collapse within himself. "Come in," she said and led him into the front room.

"Please bring us two coffees, Johannes," she asked softly of a black man who was standing just inside the doorway.

"You must be Adrian?" she asked as she motioned him to sit.

Adrian was screwing his hat into a tube. He nodded.

They chatted awhile, the niceties. Eventually Adrian came to the point, "I need to join my commando," he said, "but I was hoping to see her before I left."

"Where will you go?" she asked.

"To join De La Rey at Kraaipan."

"You should do what a man must do," Becky told him, "but you must decide what is most important to you right now." She could see the turmoil in his mind.

"So, do you think I should ride back to Kameelbult?"

"No no no," said Becky quickly, "you have to decide for yourself. I am a woman, what do I know." She never told him that she was Jewish.

Adrian looked at her closely, "but a wise woman. Now I am asking you, what do you think I should do?"

"I can only confirm what you are thinking and what you feel in your heart. De La Rey can do without you for a few days. I have heard that he has already taken the armoured train and gun. I think you could join him in a few days' time, Send your commando under your second-in-command."

Becky studied his face. He was staring at her. She looked down at her clasped hands in her lap. "Don't forget, I am only a woman. What do I know? You must decide what your priority is."

"Thank you, Aunty," he said, standing up

She stood up in front of him and held out her arms to him. She clasped him and whispered in his ear, "go to her." For some reason she could feel the tears on her cheeks.

As they parted, she wiped her cheeks with the back of her hands, "I hope to see you both again."

Adrian nodded, turned and almost ran from the room.

The road to Kameelbult was a silver ribbon in the moonlight as Adrian thundered eastward.

CHAPTER 36

After slipping across the border back into the Transvaal one night, Johan met with Pieter and Kobus. Johan needed corn, *mielies*, for planting. They loaded the bags onto a wagon in the moonlight. All went well and before daybreak they were wading out of the shallows on the Mozambique side of the river. They stopped for breakfast and were just swilling the coffee grounds out of their mugs when a Swazi rider came thundering into the camp. Johan and the others stood up.

"The farm has been raided!" he shouted, pulling his horse around in a swirl of dust.

Johan ran to him and grabbed the reins, "anyone hurt? What about my wife?"

"No, all are fine. Everyone hid when the raid started but they have driven off your breeding herd."

Johan left him and ran for his horse. The other men were already in the saddle, coffee forgotten. Johan's small breeding herd of cattle was the beginning of a future for the farm. The wagon with the corn would follow on behind.

Helena and her Swazi maid met them as they rode into the farmyard at noon. Those who had been left at the farm when Johan and his men had left for the Transvaal, two old men, women and children, were handing the riders water bags and provisions. One of the riders changed horses.

"They rode directly North," said one of the old men, "it was Sheba, I recognized him. He has a fort about half a day's ride North but turn slightly toward the coast when you think you are halfway there."

Johan swung down and hugged Helena. He had been so worried about her and just to see her hustling around handing provisions to the men felt like a waterfall of relief. All the way home he had imagined what would happen to her if she had been captured. Within minutes they were pushing their horses away, the sun on their left. The Swazi trackers were ahead but the trail was easy to follow where the small herd of cattle had flattened the grass.

As the old man had suggested, the men turned toward the coast with the sun a couple of fingers above the Lebombo mountains. The sun was setting when they spotted a barrier or wall ahead. It was a village surrounded by a wall built of tall logs, sharpened at the top.

They made camp a short distance from the wall. Far enough so that a muzzle-loader ball wouldn't reach them and in a slight dip of land. More men from the village near to Johan's farm had caught up with them. Not all of the men had horses, so it had taken them a bit longer to reach them. Enough men now to surround the village.

The real reason that these men had taken so long to reach Johan's position was that two of the leaders were resolving a grudge. The one, Obano, felt that his counterpart, Amasa, had taken part in the killing of Obano's son just at the time when Johan had taken over the farm. Obano had brought the matter to Johan but, once again, Johan had been engrossed in other things and so, had failed to act. Now with the present happenings, Obano saw a chance to take revenge and cover it up with the raid.

Just before they were about to ride out to join Johan, in the confusion, Obano called Amasa to him. Horses were milling around; the air was full of dust.

"Are you ready!" called Obano above the confusion.
He kept his voice fairly indistinct, forcing Amasa to come in close. Obano lifted his left arm, as if to embrace Amasa. Amasa came in for the embrace.

"My friend, I have wanted to do this for a long time."

As they embraced, Obano pulled a long knife. Amasa saw it but for some reason, took no notice of it. Obano pushed it into Amasa's gut. Up into his heart. Amasa stiffened and rose up onto his toes as if trying to rise above the knife. He looked deep into Obano's eyes and saw the hatred there.

As Amasa dropped away, Obano pulled himself into his saddle, "let's ride!" he shouted above all the noise. Amasa's body lay in the dust unnoticed. It was only when they were well on their way that one of the men rode alongside Obano.

"Amasa is not with us!" he shouted.

Obano reined in, "ride back and find him." They needed to wait for the men on foot anyway.

When they reached Johan, Obano told Johan that Amasa had been killed in the raid. Johan was a bit confused by this news. He was sure that he had seen Amasa walking around before his crew had ridden out. But he had other things on his mind now.

There was a river running in front of the wall. I suppose it acted like a moat. The men slept on the far bank and at daybreak started building a temporary bridge across the river. I don't know if the bridge would have held because before they got very far, an old woman came to the top of the wall and called to them.

"Why are you doing this," she called.

Johan stepped cautiously forward, "Sheba stole my cattle."

The woman disappeared behind the wall and Johan's men carried on with the bridge.

Awhile later the woman appeared again, "are you going to kill an old woman and her children?"

"Give us the cattle and Sheba and we will be on our way," called Johan.

"The cattle are being held some way north of here and as for Sheba, I will give him to you."

"Very well," said Johan and turned to Pieter, "tell the men to wait. I will see if she is good to her word. In the meantime, take ten men and scout north of here to see if the cattle are there."

"What are you going to do with Sheba?" asked Pieter.

"We can question him to see if the report about him is true."

Pieter pulled the men back from the bridge and sent Kobus with ten men to look for the cattle. Johan and the rest of the men pulled back to behind the ridge and waited.

It was hot and humid in the valley behind the ridge. It usually is hot and humid in Mozambique. A honey of a climate for breeding anopheles' mosquitoes, the ones that carry malaria.

The sun was dead overhead when Kobus came back with the news that cattle had been found with only a few herd boys watching them. Kobus had told his men to drive the cattle straight home. Still they waited with nothing happening. The sun was nearing the mountains in the west when there was a stirring behind the wall.

Johan's sentry came to call them and Johan moved forward with his men again. The woman's head could be seen above the wall. Johan made ready to take Sheba captive when, suddenly, a round shape like a football, came flying over the wall., completely over the river. Johan's men took cover. Football hadn't reached Mozambique yet.

After a few minutes, one of the men went forward and peered at it then picked it up. It was a head. The man held it high, "Sheba!" he shouted.

Johan stepped forward and waved to the old woman who then disappeared.

Johan turned, "let's go home!" he shouted.

CHAPTER 37

Approximately two thousand years ago, the centurion had just lay down on his cot. The centurion had soaked in a bath, thinking about that Jew who had died up on the mound of rotting filth. He towelled himself down with a rough, clean towel. He had witnessed death and faced death many times but this afternoon had unnerved him, for some strange reason.

It was early morning two days later and he was still trying to shake this from his mind, when a soldier knocked on the doorpost of the centurion's quarters.

"What is it now?" he scowled.

The soldier was fidgeting, "spit it out man!" the centurion shouted.

"Centurion, please come quickly."

The centurion was already pulling his tunic over his head and dragging his sandals to his bedside.

"The body has gone missing," said the soldier.

The centurion paused mid-stride. He didn't need to ask, he knew.

A rich Jew had requested the body and the governor had given permission for the body to be handed over for burial in a new, private tomb.

"Be very careful," the Jewish Sanhedrin had warned. "This is a plot by his followers to give the appearance that he has risen from the dead."

"Block the entrance to the tomb and post a guard," Pilate, the governor, had ordered.

The soldiers had carried the body to the tomb, the centurion not wanting to lose sight of the body. He had watched as the women had come to wash the blood from the body, sometimes sobbing uncontrollably. It was difficult not to be slightly moved by the process. The rich man had dressed the body with herbs before wrapping it in linen. He then rolled a boulder in front of the mouth of the tomb. Pilate had ordered the centurion personally to put a seal on the tomb. Only then did he leave the scene.

"Next you will be telling me that there are ghosts walking around town."

The soldier stopped, "about that Centurion."

The centurion grunted and walked on.

When they arrived at the garden where the tomb was situated, only two of the five soldiers were still there. They quickly came to attention alongside the soldier who had volunteered to go call the centurion.

"Why are there only three of you?" he asked them.

They remained ramrod at attention but he could see they were rattled. He couldn't understand what was going on. These were men who had fought alongside him. He knew them to be 'supposedly' fearless.

"What is the matter with you lot?" he spat out.

"Centurion, we don't know," said the first soldier, "we are sure amongst ourselves, that we did not fall asleep. We only realised at daybreak that the rock had been rolled away. We immediately looked inside the tomb but the body was gone. Only the three women were here with the spices for the body. They wouldn't have had the strength to move the rock and they were just as surprised as we were."

"Well it didn't roll itself away," said the centurion.

The soldiers looked petrified.

"You realise this means my head as well as yours."

The centurion paced up and down in front of them. Finally, he said, "go to Golgotha. Find a body that is ripe and unrecognizable. Spread the rumour that this man's followers had stolen the body but you have recovered it. Show it around and then dump it again. Then report to me again."

The soldiers ran off and after a final look round, the centurion sat down on an outcrop of rock overlooking the tomb. The morning dragged on. Nobody came back to the tomb except for the women who had accompanied this man to the cross. And there was the gardener who spoke to the women. The Centurion couldn't hear what was said. The soldiers never returned.

The gardener was talking to one of the women as the centurion sat. He sat a while thinking what he should do next. Pilate and even Herod were going to throw their toys out their cot when they heard of this. Hopefully, the soldiers had done what he had told them to do with a body from Golgotha.

Rome seemed so far away. He looked at the open tomb and then at the gardener talking to the women. The hair stood up on the back of his neck. Surely something supernatural of significance had happened here today, something that would be remembered for a while.

CHAPTER 38

Rachel felt as if her heart was breaking. They kept on missing each other. Was this fate that they shouldn't be together? But she didn't believe in fate. Maybe her God didn't want her to marry a gentile. She walked slowly down to the river. The moon was shining on the river, turning it into a silver ribbon. She lifted the hem of her dress away from the mud and sat down on a fallen trunk that she had sat on so many times while growing up.

She didn't know what to do or even think. She just let her mind wander but a picture of Adrian was always there. He had left before she could tell him how she felt. He was still a wanted man. He was also a gentile. Even if they did get together, he would never be accepted in her community.

She didn't realize how long she sat there. She didn't know that her mother was watching her from the shadows, her heart aching for her daughter. There was no advise she could give her that wouldn't turn into a disaster. Rachel hadn't told her that she loved Adrian but Ruth had watched them grow up together. Had seen the way they looked at each other and with the comings and goings of her and Adrian, as a mother, had guessed what was going on.

When Rachel came to her senses, it was just before dawn. The birds hadn't started their chatter yet. In the stillness she could hear the far-of clatter of hooves. A rider pushing his horse to the limit. Rachel turned on the fallen trunk and her mother melted away, deeper into the shadows.

The far-off clatter turned into a thunder up to the black garden gate. Adrian slid over the tree trunk and Rachel came into his arms. Nothing mattered anymore. Everything would resolve itself. Surely the God of love would help them find a way.

Rachel pulled her lips away so that she could speak and, of course, she was running out of air.

"Where you go, I will go; and where you stay, I will stay: your people will be my people; and your God my God: Where you die, I will die and there will I be buried: the Lord do so to me and more also, if anything but death part you and I."

Of course, she was quoting the Ruth of the Bible. But that Ruth wasn't a Jew. That Ruth of the Bible was a Moabite. By saying these words, Ruth had become a Jew and now Rachel, through the same process became a Christian. Accepting the fact that Jesus Christ lived and died for the specific purpose of reconciling us to God and so giving those who believed in him eternal life.

Adrian left Kameelbult the next morning for battle. He did survive the war though and came back to Kameelbult at the end of it to marry Rachel. So, Rachel became a Christian. Her father took a long time to accept this. Her mother walked around with a permanent smile which became wider when they told her that Rachel was pregnant.

We are not sure what became of Trudi or Cisca although we know that they were both at the wedding. The *Dominee* was very mindful and sensitive to the situation during the service and the baptism, quoting often from the old testament of the Jews.

Johan was overjoyed when he heard the news in Mozambique. He slipped across the border for the wedding. Oh, I did tell you that Johan and Helena had another baby boy. What I didn't tell you was that when it was born, the Prophet was at the birth. He blessed the baby.

"Your God has blessed this boy," he said to Johan and Helena, "he will lead a blessed life because your God has forgiven you. Not because anything you have done but only because He loves you."

They named the boy Jedidiah as the Prophet had said they should.

Johan had to go in disguise to the wedding. The English were still looking for him. As a precaution, Helena stayed at home. Adrian had signed a declaration at the end of the war, swearing allegiance to the queen. Johan had refused to sign and so was banned from the country. Many Boers left to live in Mozambique and Madagascar after the Second Boer War., refusing to live under British rule.

THE END

Everyone in the world is just an ordinary person. Some people may wear fancy hats or have big titles or (temporarily) have power and want you to think they are above the rest. Don't believe them. They have the same doubts, fears, and hopes; they eat, drink, sleep, and fart like everyone else. Question authority always but be wise and careful about the way you do it.

Extract from James' letter

Greater love hath no man than this, that a man lay down his life for his friends.

John 15: 13

Printed in Great Britain
by Amazon